I0703538

Playthings - A Collection of Curious Tales

Nina Mason

Copyrights©2025

All Rights Reserved

Nina Mason

Acknowledgement

For the strange

About The Author

Nina Mason is a debut author, and *Playthings - A Collection of Curious Tales* is her first published work. She completed both her bachelor's and master's degrees in literature at the University of Liverpool. Since graduating in 2019, she has worked in public sector roles.

Nina's love for all things strange, uncanny, dark, and magical is evident in her writing, which you will experience in these tales. When she's not exploring castles and haunted buildings, you can find her at home in Cheshire, England, with her partner and their two black cats.

Contents

Shadow Creatures

When he was little, Ash's grandpa would make shadow creatures with his hands before bedtime. With deft movements, he could make birds fly. And each night, Ash would be more enchanted than the last, as they fluttered across his bedroom wall. But above all else, it was his grandpa's face which he'd gaze at unblinking, as if hypnotised. He'd study the brown, leathery skin, as if it were a map of ancient isles long forgotten in the passage of time. All the while, the old head would grow larger and smaller, becoming real and unreal, in the shadows it cast.

In his youth, Ash's grandpa had been a sailor, voyaging to distant, exotic lands. Shadow puppetry was his clever trick to lull fellow sailors to sleep as they watched with heavy eyes, swaying gently in their hammocks. He would regale Ash with tales of those seafaring days, singing shanties and drumming out rhythms with his gnarled, tobacco-stained fingers.

As age caught up with him and he grew too weak to sail, his stories became his most treasured possession. He often promised Ash they would sail together one day, but that promise was never fulfilled.

After his grandpa passed, Ash had dreams of them sailing together. Yet, as the years slipped by, the wonder-filled boy transformed into a weary young man. He never learned to sail, showed little interest in girls or parties, and rarely left the house. His only pastime was taking long, meandering walks through the meadows surrounding his home, often returning late at night, long after his parents had gone to bed.

Sometimes he'd take the dog and talk to her, or throw a ball and watch her disappear into the distance as she chased after it. Other times, he'd go alone and talk to his grandpa, imagining his responses. Something about the wisdom of experience put his young nerves at rest.

On the eve of his eighteenth birthday, nine years after his grandpa's death, he went on his longest walk yet. It took him as far as the edge of the meadows, where the marshes began, so that when he looked back, the house was nothing more than a white triangle floating on a sea of green.

By the time he got home, it was dark, and the only light in the house glowed dimly in his bedroom window. His parents often left a lamp on to guide him home, like a lighthouse to guide a ship. He left his wet shoes outside and went upstairs. As he went past his parents' room, he heard nothing on the other side of the door. If his bed hadn't been freshly made, he would have thought he was alone.

The crisp white sheets were pleasantly cold to the touch. He couldn't remember falling asleep, but at some point, a sound woke him. A creaking floorboard. Perhaps one of his parents had got up, he thought, and closed his eyes again. Then he heard another creak. This time it was louder and more like a groan.

But before he could peel the bedcovers back, he realised that the sound was not coming from the floorboards but from his bed, which was rocking, ever so gently, from side to side. He knew it didn't make sense, but it seemed to, in those foggy moments between waking and sleeping.

In between the creaking came another sound, like that of wings beating. *Could it be my heart?* he thought. Normally, the dog would bark if she heard wind or thunder outside, but she hadn't stirred.

Suddenly, the beating grew louder, more insistent, jolting him upright as he called out. No voice answered. Instead, an oppressive silence seeped into every corner of the room, heavy and alive, pressing against him like a tangible force.

On the wall before him, a shadow loomed an enormous bird with wings outstretched, poised as if ready to take flight. Then, in a single sweeping motion, its vast wings enveloped him. The bedsheets whipped and billowed around him, like ship sails caught in a storm, until the relentless beating stopped.

'Sail to me,' a raspy voice whispered from far away.

'But how?' Ash replied, his breath becoming mist before his eyes.

'Just follow the moonlight,' it replied.

There was something in the voice which Ash recognised but couldn't place. Like a face in a dream. With heavy legs, he stumbled out of bed and followed the moonlight along the landing and down the stairs. It had pooled in the hallway, where a small, circular window in the front door had let it flood in. He turned the key in the lock, startled to find that it was already open, and saw that the meadow surrounding the house was submerged under water. Almost as if the moon had pulled the tide too far in.

'There's no boat,' he said, tearfully.

'Then swim.'

The whisper carried across the water's surface, dark and still, like a mirror under the sky. He looked down and saw his own reflection shatter as he slowly began to wade into its depths. First, it swallowed his knees, then his torso, and last, his head.

The next day, Ash's mother was standing beside his bed, folding the sheets, when his father walked in.

'He's not here, he must have gone out for a walk,' he said.

'I'll leave the light on so that he can find his way home,' she said, and reached for the switch.

The House That Binds

1

Nobody knew where the doll's house came from or who it had belonged to before it was put in the attic.

From the matchsticks used to frame its windows to the coconut hair used to thatch its roof, it appeared to be handmade. Fixed to its right-hand side was a latch, and at the bottom of the roof, a small, rusted padlock.

The family moved in at the end of a long, wet summer and quickly began making the place their own. When Lucie was bored one particularly dreary afternoon, she went up the narrow wooden staircase leading to the attic and found the doll's house nestled amidst pieces of furniture cloaked in old bedsheets. It was neither hidden nor in plain sight but waiting patiently to be found, like a child playing hide and seek.

What little sunlight there was shone through the single attic window and illuminated the huddle of objects that had been stored up there by previous owners. The doll's house, with its chalk-white walls and red door, was the most eye-catching of them all. And Lucie felt as though she had seen it before, though she couldn't quite remember where.

As she moved closer, she noticed that the house was sitting on a square board that had been made to look like a walled garden, with grass on either side of a cobbled path leading up to it. Around the edges of the board were dried cuttings of some sort of plant, which looked as if they'd been burned. She brought one to her nose and recoiled as its heavy musk entered her nostrils.

Tracing the edges of the window panes with her fingertip, she wondered why the house looked so familiar. And then it occurred to her that it was eerily like her new home, although with some differences.

The doll's house had a thatched roof, while the real house had a slate roof. And the real house didn't have a garden but a long driveway instead. But the thing that distinguished them the most was that the doll's house had a red front door with a number 5 on it, while the real house was number 9 and had a black front door.

Resting on her knees and gripping the front of the house with both hands, Lucie tried to pry it open, but the latch held fast. Taking a closer look at the lock that held the roof shut, she noticed that it was brass-coloured with faint engravings of intertwined leaves that had been worn away by the many hands that had touched them over the years.

She thought the key for it was probably long gone, slipped between some floorboards or taken by whoever the house once belonged to. But children have a knack for finding their way into places, with or without keys. So, she ran down the attic stairs to find her father and ask him if he had anything that could help her open the lock.

"Lucie, what have I told you about going up there? This is an old house—there are leaky pipes, loose floorboards. I don't want you hurting yourself," he said while lying on his back under the kitchen sink, with just his legs sticking out.

"I'm nine, Dad, I can handle it. And besides, you're the one who said I should get to know my new surroundings."

"Yes, but I thought you could make some new friends. The family that lives a couple of houses down—don't they have a daughter about your age?"

"She's a teenager, Dad. And what if I don't want any new friends?"

He didn't reply, so with that she sighed and went to find her mother, who was on the phone in the study.

"A doll's house with a lock? I'm sorry, could you wait a second? Lucie's here. You know what they're like." She fumbled through some papers on the desk next to her and passed a paperclip to Lucie before smiling the way she always did when she was in the middle of something and didn't want to be disturbed.

"Oh, Lucie, have you seen my locket?" her mother asked just as Lucie was leaving the room.

"Nope," Lucie replied, shrugging her shoulders.

"Never mind, I'm sure it'll be somewhere." Then she continued her conversation with whoever was on the other end of the phone.

When Lucie was a baby, her father had given her mother a silver locket with two photographs inside it—one of him and her on their wedding day and one of Lucie on her first birthday. Her mother usually wore it on a necklace but sometimes left it on her nightstand before bed or on the bathroom sink when she was showering. She always said that, after Lucie and her father, it was the third most precious thing to her.

Going back up to the attic, Lucie knelt down once more and bent the paperclip into a long, sharp pick to open the lock with. After a few unsuccessful attempts, she gave in, thinking that perhaps it was so old it was rusted shut forever. So, she tried the latch again. Using all her strength, she gripped the latch and pulled until she almost fell backwards, before it suddenly sprang loose with a high-pitched chime, and the front of the house creaked open. But before she could look inside, her father called up from downstairs.

"Lucie, what have I told you about going up there?" he said before starting to climb the attic stairs.

He reached the attic doorway to find his daughter sitting beside what appeared to be a miniature version of their new home. How strange, he thought. But if it would keep Lucie occupied, then he and her mother could get on with house repairs.

"Come on, I'll take it downstairs for you," he said, picking the house up and supporting its weight with both arms.

He set it down on top of a chest of drawers in her bedroom, where under better light she could examine it more closely.

The inside was intricately detailed, with tiny pictures on the walls, clocks with microscopic numbers, logs in the fireplaces, books on the shelves, and a bedroom that Lucie would have loved to call her own. It had a double bed with a canopy, a reading nook by the window, a huge wardrobe full of clothes, and a chest overflowing with toys. But what she liked most of all were the three little figures—a man, a woman, and a girl—who lived in the house.

The man was standing in the kitchen, arm lifted as if about to open one of the cupboards. The woman was positioned at a paper-strewn desk in the study, with a typewriter and a lamp resting on it. The girl sat in the reading nook, her head turned towards the window. *It's funny,* Lucie thought. *This family kind of reminds me of ours.*

All three had cloth bodies and hand-stitched clothes. Their faces appeared to be moulded from clay that had been delicately painted. Whoever had made them had clearly taken great care.

"Who made you?" Lucie asked, turning the girl in her hand.

She looked at the lock again. Perhaps it had been put there by the person to whom the house was given. She felt sure it was a gift. Or perhaps by whoever had made it. Whoever it was, why didn't they want the attic to be opened? Surely the house was meant to be played with.

She played with the house until teatime and afterwards fell asleep on top of her bed covers.

At some point in the night, she was awoken by her parents arguing, followed by a door slamming and someone going downstairs. It used to happen in the house they lived in before, and she felt that they might have moved to try and fix the problem, but it didn't seem to have worked.

She closed her eyes and turned over, hoping that whatever they were arguing about would resolve itself by morning.

Just as she'd started to drift off, the glow of a warm yellow light roused her. As she rubbed her eyes and lifted her head off the pillow, she saw that the doll's house was lit from inside. Although, she couldn't remember having seen any wires or switches that would make it light up.

She edged towards the house before opening its front. Then she saw that the figures had moved from the places she had last put them. The man was sitting in a chair beside the fireplace in the living room, though she was sure she'd left him in the kitchen.

The woman was in the en suite bathroom, when she had last been in the living room. And the girl was standing in her bedroom, looking towards the door.

"Lucie, are you awake?" she heard her mother's voice say from behind her. Lucie jumped, not expecting to see her there, as she hadn't heard anyone walk across the landing or open her bedroom door.

"Mum, you scared me," she said, her heartbeat quickening.

She couldn't see her mum's face, just the outline of her in the doorway, while she stood there for a few seconds silently.

"Be a good girl and go back to sleep," she said, before turning and walking back along the landing to her own room.

Lucie watched through the gap in the door as her mother disappeared into the darkness. Then she looked back towards the house and felt the tiny hairs on the back of her neck stand up. The figure of the woman was now standing on the landing, looking towards the girl's bedroom.

That's not possible, she thought. *I didn't touch it.* And she ran downstairs to find her father sitting in the living room by the fireplace.

"Dad, the people in the house—they moved on their own without me touching them."

He was slumped in his seat, with a glass in his hand. Lucie had seen him like this before in the other house. He'd always get drowsy and slur his words when he'd been drinking.

"Lucie... you were playing with that house all afternoon... are you sure it wasn't you?" He didn't look at her as he said this but was instead mesmerised by the flames dancing in the hearth.

"No, Dad, I'm certain it wasn't me. Can you come and look?" she said, gesturing towards the stairs.

"No can do, I'm afraid. It's way past somebody's bedtime." He looked at her as he said this, with a wry smile on his lips, and didn't take his eyes off her as she waited, hoping he'd change his mind.

"Ugh, goodnight, Dad," she said, and went back upstairs to her bedroom.

She didn't want to take her eyes off the doll's house in case something moved again. So, she sat in bed, watching it for as long as she could fight her tiredness, before her eyelids became too heavy and she fell asleep.

2

The next day, the rain had cleared. Lucie woke to find the figures in the doll's house in the same positions she had left them the night before. The woman was in the living room, the man in the kitchen, and the girl lying on her bed. *Perhaps I imagined they'd moved,* Lucie thought.

She got out of bed and went across the landing to her parents' room, where she could see her mum sitting in the en suite, with the door slightly ajar. She was looking down at something in her hands, with tears in her eyes.

"Morning, Mum," Lucie said, bursting in. Her mother stood up quickly and turned so that her back blocked the door.

"Lucie, you can't just barge in here like that. Go and get some breakfast. There's some cereal in the cupboard and milk in the fridge. I'll be down soon."

"What's that you're holding?"

"It's just my toothbrush. Now, can I have some privacy, please?"

Lucie went downstairs and got herself some cereal, though there was no milk left, so she ate it dry out of the packet. Then she went across the hall into the living room.

A pile of ashes lay in the fire grate, and the cushions on the chair looked as if someone had been sitting on them.

Then she heard someone whistling outside the front window. She went into the hall and opened the front door. There was her father, dressed in white overalls, crouching to open a tin of paint.

"What are you up to, Dad?" she asked, gently rocking on her heels.

"I'm giving this door a lick of paint," he said. "Never did like the colour black."

She watched him dip a paintbrush into the tin and lift it, letting two blobs of bright red paint drip over the edge.

"I'll have to nip to the shops," her mother said, as she came out of the house and unlocked the car. "There's no milk left, and we'll need more food to keep us going for the rest of the week."

While she was watching her mother reverse out of the driveway, Lucie was acutely aware of an old woman standing on the other side of the street, watching her. The woman had grey hair in ringlets at her shoulder, wore a lilac cardigan, and had a troubled expression on her face.

Curious to find out why she was standing there, Lucie walked over to her.

"Hello, my name's Lucie. We've just moved into number 9," she said in her best voice.

The old woman's gaze had been fixed on the house while Lucie spoke. Then, when she'd finished, the woman looked at her with her big, watery blue eyes and said, "Pleasure to meet you, Lucie. I'm Iris, and I've lived at number 4 since I was a girl, just like you."

Iris seemed unsteady on her feet, pushing down on the handle of a crooked walking stick with both hands, as if to steady herself. So, Lucie asked if she wanted to come inside for a glass of homemade lemonade and a place to sit.

"That's very kind of you, but if you wouldn't mind, I'd rather we sit in the garden," Iris said.

The weather was much brighter than it had been yesterday, and there were a couple of garden chairs for them to use. So, Lucie helped Iris up the driveway and brought her a cold glass of lemonade.

"You're too kind," Iris said. "I hope you don't think I'm rude for wanting to sit outside. It's just that... I promised I'd never set foot in Thornwick again." As she spoke, she glanced over her shoulder at the house, then clasped her hands to her chest and leaned forward, as if she was hiding something from it.

"Thornwick?" Lucie asked, confused.

Iris nodded, nervously fiddling with the pearl buttons on her cardigan. "That's what the locals called this place—the first house ever built in this village, made from the wood of the black forest that once stood here," she said. "Though I'm the only soul living who remembers."

"Why won't you go in the house?" Lucie asked.

There was a pause.

"Many years ago, my childhood friend Agatha—Aggy, as we used to call her—lived in your house. She was a lovely girl. Always laughing and smiling," Iris said, a sorrowful look in her eyes. Her voice grew quieter. "Oh, but her family had problems. There were always arguments. Then one day, she told me about this man upstairs who gave her a doll's house that looked just like Thornwick. Well, she was never the same after that."

"Never the same?"

"The light went out of her eyes. One day, her father found her in the attic, trying to burn Thornwick to the ground. That's when he locked that thing up, and the family moved away from the village. But by then, it was too late for poor Aggy."

"What happened to her?"

Tears began to roll down Iris's cheeks. "They took her to an institution for the mentally afflicted. They thought she must have been experiencing hallucinations—that she was delusional and obsessed with religion—because she kept talking about 'the man upstairs'. The last I heard of her was so long ago I can scarcely remember. They called to tell me she'd passed, but I felt her spirit return the day you moved into that house. She came to warn me about you."

"About me?"

"He can sense an unhappy child like a spider senses a fly tangled in its web. Aggy was the happiest girl I knew, but her parents' troubles broke her heart."

Lucie didn't know what to say. It was such an awful story, what had happened to Iris's friend. But she wasn't unhappy, and her parents didn't have any troubles. Then she remembered the night before—her parents' argument and the figures in the house that had moved, almost as if in recognition of what was happening. She thought of how her mother had hidden something from her in the bathroom that morning.

"How does he sense it?" Lucie asked tentatively.

"He has eyes everywhere, my dear. It's some sort of dark magic—older than the house itself, as ancient as the trees that were chopped down to build it."

"Can he be stopped?"

"Only love can break his spell. He'll take the things that matter to you most; you must take them back."

Iris knew about an awful lot of things. She told Lucie that she was in her eighties, but she could easily have told her that she was hundreds of years old and Lucie wouldn't have doubted it. She was wise and intuitive. She could see that Lucie was harbouring resentment about the house move and her parents' arguments. And she sensed a kind of rivalry from Lucie that you don't often see in a family with one child.

After they'd finished their lemonades and the sun had gone in, Lucie walked Iris to the end of the driveway.

"Well, it's been nice speaking with you, Iris. I hope we'll see each other again soon."

"Same to you, my dear. And don't forget—find the things he took from you," she said, pointing a bony, arthritic finger at Lucie.

Lucie watched as Iris shuffled across the street and entered her house. She appeared in one of the downstairs windows but quickly drew the curtains. *She must have me confused with her friend,* Lucie thought. *I don't know about dark magic.* Still, no matter how much she tried to dismiss Iris' words as the ramblings of a confused old woman, deep down, Lucie feared Iris wasn't mistaken at all.

While Lucie had been talking with Iris, her mother had returned from the shops, and her father had finished painting the front door.

Lucie went straight upstairs to her bedroom to check on the doll's house. Nothing had moved. Talking with Iris had made her superstitious; she closed the front of the house and pushed the rusted latch back into place, securing it shut. She resolved to ask her father to put the house back in the attic when she got the chance.

"You were with that old lady for quite a while," her father said during lunch. "What were you two talking about?"

"Her name's Iris. She had a friend who used to live here, but something awful happened to her."

Lucie's parents waited, anticipating what their young daughter would say next. They'd been told before buying the property that there'd been a fire in the 1860s, back when the house had its original thatched roof, later replaced with slate. They also knew the house used to be number five before becoming number nine when another property was built between it and the neighbouring house in the 1920s. This had all been revealed to them by the previous landlady, whose tenants had left abruptly, leaving it vacant for almost a year.

Lucie's parents were not locals. They'd been looking for somewhere to give them the time and space to work on their marriage and hopefully grow their family. They had always planned for a second child, but the doctors had told them their chances of conceiving again were very slim. This had taken a toll on her mother, which in turn, had led to her father drinking. They didn't want Lucie growing up in an unhappy home, but their own struggles made it hard to put on a brave face.

Since moving in, Iris had been the only neighbour to approach them. Lucie's father had noticed her watching the house from across the street several times. He'd waved, but Iris, her eyes distant as though lost in thought, never waved back.

"Did you know our house has a name, Dad?" Lucie asked.

"It does?"

"Thornwick. Iris said there used to be a forest here."

"Well, that explains why this place is so strong and sturdy," he said, chuckling as he rapped on a wooden beam in the kitchen with his knuckles.

"And she said my doll's house used to belong to her friend," Lucie added.

"Did her friend enjoy playing with it as much as you do?" her father asked with a smile.

"I'm not sure I should play with it anymore, Dad."

"Why's that?"

"She said a man gave it to her friend, and then bad things started happening."

"Sounds like she was just telling you a load of old nonsense. Is that why you were in the attic earlier, trying to put the doll's house back?"

"No, Dad, I haven't been in the attic today."

He shook his head, standing to wash his plate in the sink. "I could have sworn I heard someone moving about up there," Lucie heard him mutter under his breath.

"Don't look at me—I've been out all afternoon," her mother said, catching the end of their conversation.

Had her father misheard the usual creaks and knocks of the old house? A mouse scratching? Or had someone really been up there? Lucie wondered.

She needed to know. While her father worked in the garden and her mother wallpapered downstairs, Lucie crept upstairs to the attic.

The furniture, cloaked in bedsheets, still stood there, huddled together like ghosts at a secret meeting. She wouldn't have been able to tell if anything had shifted since the day before.

Standing on tiptoes, she peered out of the attic window. From there, she had a clear view of Iris' house. *I wonder why she keeps all her curtains closed during the day*, Lucie thought.

Just then, she lost her balance and fell, pulling the cover off a mirror propped against a chair. As she sat up, rubbing dust from her eyes, she noticed something reflected behind the furniture in the mirror.

In the far-right corner of the attic, under the eaves, sat a bed and a brass candle holder atop a wooden nightstand. The stub of a candle inside had melted into long, tapering shapes like fingers. Beside it were a pair of scissors, a needle, a spool of thread, some newspaper clippings, and strands of brown hair.

The bed was made, as though someone had recently slept in it. Unlike the rest of the attic, it wasn't dusty.

Then Lucie thought she saw something move under the bed. She reached down to lift the edge of the cover but stopped as voices drifted up from downstairs.

She dropped the cover and hurried to the landing, crouching by the bannisters to listen.

"Are you sure?" her father's voice asked.

"Of course I'm sure. I checked again this morning," her mother replied. "When do we tell Lucie?"

"I think we should keep it quiet for a few weeks. She's been acting up lately, and I don't want to make things worse."

Lucie had suspected her mother was hiding something. Even before that morning in the bathroom, her mother had seemed distant and preoccupied. Whenever Lucie needed her—or just wanted to spend time with her—she was always too busy or too tired.

Lucie's legs tingled with pins and needles as she stayed crouched. Then she heard her mother's footsteps in the hall and quickly darted into her bedroom. While her mother entered her parents' room, Lucie fiddled with the doll's house to avoid arousing suspicion.

Something had changed. In the couple's bedroom within the doll's house, there was now a cot. Inside it lay a baby.

30

3

Lucie picked up the baby with her thumb and forefinger and brought it closer to her face. It had the same cloth body and painted face as the other figures, and she knew instantly what it meant.

"Lucie, come here right now!" her mother shouted from the other room.

Jolted by the severity of her mother's tone, Lucie dropped the baby on the floor and went to see what her mother wanted.

She opened the bedroom door and saw her mother standing there, clutching one of her nightgowns, torn to pieces.

"You know, Lucie, if you were thinking of making something for your doll's house, I would have liked you to tell me first—before taking a pair of scissors to my nightgown. What were you thinking?" her mother said, throwing the shreds of material at Lucie. "And I still can't find my locket."

"I didn't touch your nightgown or your locket, Mum."

"Do you know what, Lucie? I've had about enough of your attention-seeking. If you wanted my attention, this was not the way to get it."

"But, Mum, I—"

"Enough! Get to your room. And you needn't think you'll be staying up playing with that doll's house."

Lucie's mother took her by the shoulders and hurried her along the landing to her room, then picked up the house and left, slamming the door behind her.

Tears of frustration welled up in Lucie's eyes. She looked at the baby on the floor and stamped on it again and again before collapsing in a heap on her bed.

Maybe Iris was right, she thought. Bad things had happened to Aggy when she played with the house, and bad things had been happening to her ever since she found it.

She buried her head in her pillow as she heard her mother's footsteps go back down the stairs, followed by raised voices.

Her mother told her father about the torn nightgown, her concerns over Lucie's attention-seeking behaviour in recent weeks, and how her obsession with the doll's house was becoming a problem.

Then, the doorbell rang.

"Oh no, who could that be?" her mother muttered, irritated that someone had turned up unexpectedly.

"I'll get it," her father said.

As he opened the door, he saw Iris craning her neck to look at the roof of the house, leaning on her stick for support.

"Sorry, can I help you?" he asked, stepping out briefly and following her gaze.

"Do excuse me," Iris replied, sensing that he might be offended. "We've never been introduced, but I met your daughter earlier, and I fear she may be in danger."

Lucie's mother had heard this from inside the house and came out to see what nonsense the old woman was peddling now.

"That doll's house of hers is no toy—it's a trap. That's how he lures them in. I know because it happened to my friend when I was a child, and I've seen the same look in your daughter's eyes as I did in hers all those years ago," Iris continued.

Lucie's parents exchanged a disbelieving look. They were about to bid her a good evening and send her on her way when, in the most nonchalant tone, she said something that made their blood run cold.

"She already knows about the baby."

They had no choice but to listen to her now. They didn't know how Lucie could have known, or why she'd confided in a perfect stranger instead of them. But they heeded Iris' words when she warned them that their daughter wasn't happy—and that things would get much worse if they allowed her to continue playing with the house. Even if they couldn't tolerate the other nonsense Iris spouted, they could agree with her on that.

Meanwhile, upstairs, Lucie had picked up the figure of the baby off the floor and was looking at it. The head had separated from the body when she stamped on it and was now hanging loosely by a couple of threads. But the material—the soft, pink cotton—she'd seen it somewhere before. Holding it to her nose, she recognised the scent—it was her mother's. The figure's body was stuffed with crumpled newspaper, which was protruding from the hole where its head had detached. But folded in with it was a lock of brown hair. Lucie pulled it out to look at it more closely.

Both her and her mother had brown hair, though her mother's hair was fine and straight, while Lucie's was thick and curly. This hair looked like it belonged to her mother.

Just then, Iris left, and Lucie's father took the doll's house from the living room where her mother had left it and put it outside. Then he went to the garage to grab an axe. What had started as a harmless way to pass the time during the long summer days had turned into an unhealthy obsession. He had to destroy the house.

Hearing all the commotion, Lucie sneaked out of her room and downstairs. She saw her father through the open front door, raising the axe above his head before striking the doll's house, making a jagged opening in the roof.

"Lucie, go back to your room," he said firmly, striding back towards the house and into the living room.

She ignored him and walked over to the doll's house. Looking down into the dark cavity in the roof, a wave of anger swept over her, and she knew at that moment that she couldn't let her father destroy the house. So, she scooped it up in her arms and ran back inside as fast as she could. When she reached the landing and stopped to open the attic door, her mother was close behind.

As Lucie lifted the house and began to climb the first few steps, her mother tried to take it from her—but she stumbled and fell.

Once inside, Lucie shut the door behind her, pushing a chair up against it and jamming the handle so no one could get in from the other side. Her mother, now on the other side, banged against the door with her fist as hard as she could.

"Lucie, open the door," she called, her voice growing more desperate with each repetition, as the door vibrated in its frame and the chair holding it shut scraped against the floorboards.

Lucie could hardly bear it any longer. She reached into the doll's house and grabbed the figure of the woman, holding the body in one hand and the head in the other. She twisted them in opposite directions.

Then, the banging stopped, and a loud, dull thud echoed from the other side of the attic door.

Lucie began to sob uncontrollably, fearing the worst. She had wanted the shouting to stop and had reached for the doll in haste but never intended to hurt her mother.

Another set of footsteps began climbing the attic staircase, and then Lucie heard her father's voice—first tearful, then frantic—as he tried to wake her mother.

He started to kick the attic door repeatedly until the hinges eventually gave way and the door burst open. It took a few seconds for his eyes to adjust to the darkness. As they did, he saw the softened silhouettes of the covered furniture and the outline of Lucie on her knees.

"Lucie?"

As his voice rang out into the silence, the wooden beam above him let out a low groan before crashing down, pulling chunks of plaster and other debris with it. Then, as the dust began to settle, a shaft of pale moonlight pierced the darkness, illuminating the far corner of the attic.

Lucie thought she saw one of the other ceiling beams move ever so slightly that it was almost imperceptible. She lingered on it a little longer before realising that, where there was once a single beam, there were now five, slowly descending from above. Blinking to reassure herself that it was just a trick of the light, Lucie came face to face with a creature that had long, flowing limbs, like tree branches in winter. As she became aware of it, it continued to move, though so slowly that it was as if time itself had stopped for a moment.

"Who are you?" she called out. There was a slight pause followed by a low hiss as the creature inhaled through clenched teeth.

"I am the one who sees," it rasped.

"You're the one who made the house, aren't you?" she asked.

The figure laughed. "Yes. You liked that, didn't you, Lucie? But mummy and daddy didn't, did they?"

"Why are you here?"

"Because you wanted to play," it said, smiling and baring its teeth that were sharp like thorns. Up close, its skin was black as ebony and knotted like tree bark. But where its eyes should have been, there were none.

"Well, I don't want to play anymore. I want my family back."

"Even though they don't love you?"

"That's not true—they do love me, and I love them."

"Ah, but you haven't broken my spell yet."

Lucie remembered what Iris had said—to take back the things he'd taken from her. But what things?

"Lucie," her father gasped, breathless.

"Dad!" she cried, rushing to him and trying with all her might to free him from the beam. As she did, she looked up and saw the wide grin of the figure, leering at her.

"Get help," her father said weakly.

Lucie stepped over the rubble and out of the attic, stopping briefly to stroke her mother's cheek. She was lying with her head to one side, breathing shallowly.

"Hang in there, Mum," Lucie said, before running down the attic stairs as fast as she could and going into her parents' room to use the phone. She tried to dial the emergency services, but the phone seemed to be disconnected. *The collapsed roof must have damaged the telephone wire*, she thought.

She left the house and ran across the street to Iris's. There were no lights on inside, and all the curtains were shut, but she was the only one who could help. Lucie started pounding the door with her fist and shouting, "Iris, please, I need your help!"

A light came on in the upstairs bedroom, and then Lucie heard someone fumbling with keys on the other side of the door.

"Lucie, dear, what's happened?" Iris asked, opening the door in her nightgown.

"I've seen him—the man upstairs. He's real, and he hurt my parents," Lucie said without stopping to take a breath.

"Oh, my dear," said Iris, reaching for Lucie's hand and squeezing it. "You must break the spell."

"But Iris, I don't understand."

Iris sighed, as though deeply disappointed by the words she was about to say. "He is a spirit from the forest that once stood where your house now stands—a prisoner bound to your house, capturing the souls of lonely, unhappy children who will share in his misery."

"You said he has lots of eyes, but he has none," Lucie said desperately.

"The dolls, my dear. Find them and the things he took from you to free your family. Go to your parents, and I'll catch up as soon as I can."

Then it all started to make sense: her mother's necklace, the lock of hair. He'd taken them and hidden them inside the dolls—they were his eyes. She had to take back the things he'd taken from them and break the spell.

As these thoughts raced through her mind, Lucie reached the attic to find her mother still lying in the doorway, breathing softly but whimpering, as if trapped in a nightmare. Her father lay silent beneath the beam, his chest rising and falling rhythmically, his eyes closed.

Clouds covering the moon made it difficult to see anything in the attic clearly. Remembering the candle she'd found up there, Lucie felt her way past the covered furniture to the nightstand and then reached inside its single drawer for some matches. As she did, she caught sight of the creature clambering silently across the ceiling towards her. She took a match from the box and struck it twice, flicking sparks into the air. The end of the match glowed faintly before burning out. She took another one from the box and struck it three times. This time, a bright yellow flame roared to life, crackling, as she used it to light the candle stub beside the bed. Then, she took the scissors and made her way back over to the doll's house, which was sitting right where she'd first found it.

Placing the candle holder on the floor beside the house, she took the figure of the woman from inside it and used the scissors to cut its head off. To Lucie's horror, her mother began thrashing violently, her body thumping against the floorboards.

"Oh, Lucie, look what you've done now," the creature jeered.

Lucie pushed her thumb and forefinger inside the figure's cloth body and felt the cold metal of her mother's lost locket before taking it out and putting it in the pocket of her jeans. Next, she took the figure of the man and opened it up to find a wallet-sized photo of her mother when she was younger. It was frayed around the edges and looked as if it had been taken in a photo booth years before Lucie was born. And lastly, she took a blue butterfly hairpin from the figure of the girl, which her mother had given to her on her birthday earlier that year.

The creature let out a loud hiss. "You'll never find the last one," it whispered in her ear, clinging to a beam above them.

"You're lying, there isn't another one. I found them all," she said, standing and turning to face it.

"They won't wake up unless you find it," the creature said, tapping its long fingernails.

What else was there? Lucie thought. As she stood contemplating, her eyes fell on the hole in the roof of the doll's house. The creature caught her looking. But how could he see if the dolls were his eyes and she'd destroyed them? Lucie wondered.

She heard someone coming up the attic stairs slowly, stopping on each step to take a breath. The creature heard them too and turned its head to see Iris standing in the attic doorway, clutching something to her chest.

"All these years I've kept you here—you promised me you wouldn't hurt another child," Iris said to the creature.

"Iris, what's going on?" Lucie asked, beginning to worry.

"We made a deal," she began to explain, "that I would let him stay at Thornwick so long as he never hurt another child the way he hurt my Aggy."

"Why don't you tell her the whole story, Iris? She's a big girl; she can handle it," the creature said, grinning.

"I never meant for any of it to happen," Iris said, beginning to sob. "I found him in the attic while we were playing hide-and-seek one day, and he told me I could live forever, as long as I made sure he could stay in this house. This is his home, you see. After the forest was destroyed, he had nowhere else to go. I was just a girl; I felt sorry for him."

"Excuses, excuses," the creature said.

"But not anymore. I've been holding onto this for a lifetime—take it and open the lock on the doll's house," Iris said, extending her fist towards Lucie and opening it to reveal a small brass key in her palm.

"I wouldn't do that if I were you," the creature warned.

Lucie approached Iris and took the key from her hand. So that's what she'd been hiding yesterday afternoon while they were talking in the garden, Lucie thought. She went over to the doll's house and knelt down, turning the key in the lock until it clicked open.

As she lifted the roof of the house, a deep, earthy scent, like that of rotting leaves, filled the air. There, in its dark little attic, was a bed, a nightstand, and the figure of a tall, thin man with no eyes or nose on his face—just a wide, toothy grin. His arms and legs were so long that they reached from one side of the attic to the other. And up and down the lengths of the wooden ceiling beams, she could see scratches, as if something or someone had dragged sharpened fingernails along them. This man, this creature, had been there all along—hidden in plain sight. It was him who her father had heard, knocking and scratching in the attic. It was him who Iris hid behind the curtains from.

Lucie grabbed the hideous doll and began tearing it to pieces. As she did, the creature which had been hanging from the eaves above her screeched and clawed at the ceiling, and then at the floorboards, as it tried to scramble away.

"His heart, Lucie. Rip out his heart," Iris cried.

Reaching inside the doll, Lucie pulled out a large, black seed. The creature lunged at her once more, letting out an awful shriek. She put her fingers in her ears and didn't take them out until the creature fell silent and began to fold in on itself, like a threatened spider, until it shrivelled up completely, leaving nothing but a dirty stain on the floorboards where it had been.

A cough came from under the pile of rubble, where the roof had caved in. Lucie's father had awoken and was trying to sit up.

"Dad!" she cried, running to his aid.

Outside, the sirens of emergency service vehicles blared in the distance. Iris had called them before she'd left her house, but now she was standing, hunched over against the back of a chair, as if in pain.

"Help is coming," Lucie told her father before going to her mother, who was awake but dazed, with a few gashes on her arms and legs from thrashing against the floorboards. Lucie noticed that Iris was struggling. "Are you okay? Here, let me help you," she said, assisting Iris into the chair.

"I've let you down, dear," Iris said, her head hung low. "I bargained with that devil when I was just a girl. And look where it got me."

"Iris, you said he promised you could live forever—you're not really in your eighties, are you?" Lucie asked.

"That was in exchange for keeping him in this house, but now he's gone, I won't last much longer. It was my one hundred and fortieth birthday this year."

That explains why she knows so much, Lucie thought. "You were young. You couldn't have known he was bad," she said, hoping to reassure her friend.

A couple of police cars and an ambulance arrived shortly after and took both Lucie's mother and father to hospital, where they were treated for their injuries from the fallen roof. Of course, they didn't know how it had all come about—only Lucie and Iris knew that.

Lucie's father had broken one of his legs, so he had to wear a cast and use crutches for several weeks. Her mother, however, recovered fully within days and shared the news about the new baby with Lucie and Iris, who did their best to look surprised.

The hole in the roof was repaired, and the family began spending more quality time together. Sadly, Iris passed away from old age a few months later. A couple with two children—a seven-year-old girl and a four-year-old boy—moved into her house.

One day the following spring, Lucie was planting flowers with the girl and her mother in their garden when she felt something in the pocket of her jeans. It was the large, black seed she had found inside the doll.

"What's that?" the girl asked.

"I think it's a tree seed," Lucie said.

"Give it to me," the girl said. "Let's plant it and see what grows.

Little One

Esther wasn't an only child, but she often felt like one. She had an elder sister named Nell, who she would sit in the garden and play picnic with, alongside their teddies who each had their own tiny cup and saucer, which Esther would kindly pour lumpy, green pond water into. The sisters would never eat any of it, of course. It was just pretend. But Nell never ate, so every teatime was pretend for her.

Their family tradition of setting Nell's place at the table, while she watched as others ate, had never struck Esther as odd until she invited a school friend over one evening.

"It's so creepy the way she stares at you," Esther heard the girl say to the other children the next day at school.

"Didn't you say she doesn't blink?" asked one of the boys.

"I've heard they sleep in the same bed," another girl said.

Esther sat with her back turned to them, picking pips out of a brown apple core, pretending that she couldn't hear them. But when she got home from school later that day, to find Nell sitting silently at the end of her bed, she thought about what the other children had said. Why didn't her sister blink? Why didn't she speak? Why didn't she eat? Why didn't she grow? Why did she need to be carried everywhere?

Deep down, Esther knew the answers to these questions. She knew that big girls didn't play silly little games. But her mother liked to.

"Esther, tea's ready. Bring your sister down!" her mother called from the kitchen.

Esther glowered at her sister before grabbing her cold, hard hand and dragging her down the stairs.

"You shouldn't be so rough with Nell, you'll pull her arm off one of these days," her mother said, while chopping some vegetables.

"Tell her," she said to the girls' father, gesturing with the knife still in her hand.

Esther glanced up from the table at her father, who gave a tight-lipped smile but remained silent. He was good at playing this game. He'd been playing it for a lot longer than she had.

Once they'd all sat down and began tucking into their meals, Esther took a piece of carrot from her sister's plate, put it in her mouth, and crunched it loudly. Nell didn't stir or complain. She just sat there with the same vacant expression that she always had. Her next birthday she'd be turning thirteen, but no one would ever have guessed. Esther was the taller of the two and had started to choose her own clothes, whereas Nell wore Esther's hand-me-downs.

When she was younger and still smaller than her sister, Esther's mother had called her "little one." She'd scoop her up in her arms, carry her to bed, and pull the quilt right up to her chin.

"Ssshhhh, the fae folk are sleeping in the forest," she'd say, pressing a finger to her lips. And Esther knew that this meant she needed to be quiet and go to sleep, because the forest was just beyond her bedroom window, and she didn't want to wake them.

Her mother told her that she'd loved the forest when she was a little girl, but Esther felt that maybe she was scared of it now because she never wanted to go in there.

"Esther Morley, don't you dare take food from your sister's plate," her mother said in a low voice.

"But don't you think it's a waste, mum? All this food that Nell can't eat."

Her mother stopped cutting her food abruptly, causing the knife and fork to screech against the plate.

"Go to your room," she said, flatly.

Esther got down from her chair and ran upstairs to her room, where she could hear her parents' muffled voices below.

"I don't know what's got into her," her mother said.

"I was hoping this day wouldn't come so soon, but I think it might be time for us to tell her about what happened to Nell," her father said softly. It was as if he was trying to gain the trust of a frightened animal, though neither one trusted the other.

Esther heard her mother reply, but she was speaking so quietly that it was impossible to make out the words. Could they be talking about all the things that her father tried to tell her about while her mother was out of the room? About how she wasn't very happy, and how sometimes unhappy people do strange things. But when did this unhappiness start?

Her mother had been playing these games for as long as she could remember. Cooking food that Nell couldn't eat, walking her in a pushchair, reading her bedtime stories, and talking to her. Loving a child that couldn't love her back. But now that Esther was growing up, it was becoming more and more difficult to play along.

Nell must have spent the night downstairs, because she wasn't sitting in her usual spot, at the end of Esther's bed, the next morning. Instead, she was outside with her father, in the garden, while her mother watched them both through the kitchen window. From a distance, Nell could be mistaken for a normal child. It was only when you got close to her that you could see she was too perfect.

"What are you doing?" Esther asked her mother.

"Oh, just making some lunch," she said, pivoting on her heels with a plate of sandwiches in her hand.

"Take these out to those two, would you sweetheart?" she asked, smiling through gritted teeth.

Esther took the plate in her hands and went outside, to find Nell sat stiffly next to her dad.

"Mum made these for you."

"Not having any?" he asked, with a sad smile. It was the one where his eyes didn't seem to match his mouth. Both her parents had this smile.

"Look, this might be hard for you to understand, but your mum's not well," he said, looking back towards the house as he spoke.

"Is she sick?"

"She just... misses her, that's all."

"Misses who?"

There was a pause, and then he said, "Nell."

"But dad—"

"There was another little girl before..."

Without finishing his sentence, he slowly moved his gaze towards the mute figure sat, straight-legged across from them.

Just then, Esther's mother came out of the house and told them that she'd seen some dark clouds drawing in and that they should come inside before the rain.

He'd said too much, and he knew it. When he went into her bedroom that night and found her wide awake, he knew she would ask about the other girl.

"What happened to her, Dad?" she asked, peeping over the covers.

There was something about the innocence in his daughter's eyes that stopped him from telling her the whole truth. Instead, he gave her half of it.

"She went into the forest to play with the fae folk, but never came back," he said, turning away from the moonlight so she couldn't see his face. Then he kissed her cheek and left the room, closing the door softly behind him.

She didn't sleep. She thought about Nell—not the glassy-eyed one sitting on the chair at the end of her bed, but the one who was out there, in the forest. Maybe the day Nell went missing was the day her mother stopped being happy. And maybe, if she brought her back, she could make her mother happy again.

Best to go before breakfast, she thought. That way, she could surprise her mother in the morning. As she put on her wellies and duffle coat over her pyjamas, all she could think of was the smile on her mother's face when she saw the real Nell again.

But this time, it would be a real smile—not the one where her eyes didn't match her mouth.

The night air was damp and settled in tiny droplets on her hair and coat as she made her way into the dense forest. She wandered as far as she could from the house, pausing now and then to glimpse its walls through the tall pines—until she could see them no longer. Once or twice, she thought she saw her mother's face in the kitchen window, searching for the child she'd lost.

58

The Third

The car crash happened when Eliot was four, going on five. His father had been driving him to school that morning when he suddenly lost control of the car, mounted the pavement, and sped into a wall. The impact killed him instantly, but Eliot, who had been sitting in the back seat, survived.

There had been a third person in the car with them that day, though Eliot could only vaguely remember—there was a man sitting in the seat beside him. He didn't say anything or move from his stiff position. He was there, and then he wasn't. Only two people were cut out of the wreckage—Eliot and his father.

The memory of the man stayed with Eliot for years. It was vivid but fragmented, like a glimmer of something that flashed in his mind sometimes without warning. This is why he named the man 'Glim'. It wasn't so much a conscious decision as a quiet understanding that this was his name. He never told anyone about

Glim, and as the years passed, the memory of him faded until it was barely there at all.

Eliot was now twenty-five—he had a steady job as a data analyst for a big tech company, his own flat, and a long-term girlfriend. Things were going well for him, though the twentieth anniversary of his father's death loomed large in his mind, like the bright headlights of a car on a dark country road.

October 9th was a day he dreaded. Each year, while growing up, his mother had retreated into herself on the anniversary of his father's death, and he had no way of consoling her. There was an unspoken resentment from her towards his father for having died and left her to raise their young son. But since she couldn't direct this towards her late husband, she unconsciously directed it towards their son.

In recent years, Eliot's relationship with his mother had been strained, and he kept their contact to a minimum—calling her once a week to see how she was doing, though it was always the same answer. But twenty years since the crash marked another milestone—a short lifetime since his father had died. He was going to have to visit her.

It was late September, and Eliot was coming up the stairs of the building he lived in, when his neighbour, an elderly Chinese lady who didn't speak much English, told him he had a visitor. After asking her a few questions, he established that while he'd been out at work, she had heard someone pressing the buzzer for his flat on the downstairs intercom but couldn't reach the front door in time to answer.

Probably a cold caller or post which wouldn't fit through the letterbox, he thought. His girlfriend Lydia would have told him if she'd stopped by, and besides, she would have been at work.

He entered his flat, hung his coat and bag on the hook behind the door, then went to the toilet, splashed some water onto his face, and looked in the mirror over the sink. He was beginning to get fine lines on either side of his mouth and across his forehead, though he still looked young for his age. His father had been thirty-two when he died and had seemed so much older.

Eliot went into the kitchen, began tidying the morning's dishes away, and cleared the kitchen surfaces so he could prepare dinner. It was then that he noticed the window was open just enough for someone to climb through it. He couldn't remember leaving it open. Each morning, before he left for work, he went through a routine of making sure all the windows were closed, the dials on the cooker were set to zero, the TV was off, and the door was locked.

Perturbed, he went to check the living room and then the bedroom to see if anything was missing. Everything was still in the places he'd left them that morning. So, he put it down to forgetfulness and started cooking dinner. Just then, he got a phone call from Lydia.

"Hey you, have you called your mum yet?" she asked.

"Well, actually, I'm kind of busy this week, so I'll call her when I get a minute," he said, knowing she wouldn't buy his excuse.

"She's just lonely—you know that's why she's so hard on you, right?"

"Yeah, I know. But it's not my fault my dad decided to drive his kid to school while he had a hangover."

There was a pause before she spoke again. "Are you still seeing your therapist?"

"Lydia, would you stop worrying? I don't need a therapist. It was twenty years ago; I can barely remember."

"Okay, well, just promise me you'll give me a call if things get tough. I know it's difficult for you this time of year."

"Will do. Anyway, I'll talk to you later. Love you." He put the phone down on the counter and saw that he had five missed calls and a voicemail from the same number.

This was becoming a regular occurrence. Every week, or every other week, for the past few months, he'd been receiving calls from unknown numbers that were sometimes followed by voicemails where nobody would speak on the other end of the phone. The buzz of white noise came through for a few seconds before the caller hung up or the voicemail was cut off. Each time it was a different number, though he'd traced a handful of them and found they were made from payphones in various locations around the city.

He picked up the phone and listened to the voicemail. For the first few seconds, it was just static, and then he heard a high-pitched voice say, "I'm here," before the voicemail cut off.

The police told him it was probably just kids playing pranks when he reported the calls. This voice sounded like a child's, but there was something deeply unsettling about the innocence of it, and the simplicity of the message the caller was delivering.

It wasn't the voice of a teenager trying to scare him with heavy breathing and hollow threats. Instead, it was like a gentle tap on the shoulder and the voice of a small child simply saying: "I'm here."

He deleted the voicemail and went to eat his dinner on the couch while half-heartedly watching a trash reality TV show. Then, afterward, he called Lydia back, who took longer than usual to answer.

"Hey, you," he said.

"Hey, what's up?" she said, sounding agitated.

"Nothing, I just thought I'd call you."

"Oh, well, I'm out with Maddy at the moment. You said you were busy this week."

He could hear voices and music in the background of the call. Lydia was the type of girl who always had a friend to call on when Eliot wasn't around. It's like she can't bear to be alone, he thought, irritated by her neediness.

"I am, but I just wanted—"

"What? I can't hear you," she said, interrupting him mid-sentence.

"I got another one of those calls," he said loudly.

"...Sorry, El, I can't hear you."

"Where are you?" he asked.

"I'm—." The line went dead. He sat watching the animated facial expressions of the people on TV as they argued without sound, the phone still in his hand.

Is she seeing someone? he thought to himself. Some of Lydia's friends had boyfriends, but he only knew them in passing—maybe it was one of them. The thought lingered in his mind until he fell asleep on the couch, the blue light from the TV screen flickering in the dark flat.

The following morning, he woke up late for work and had to rush to make it in on time. He spent the day tired and unable to focus. Thoughts of Lydia's possible infidelity, having to visit his mother, and getting through the anniversary of his father's death weighed on him heavily.

He thought of visiting his mother and drove by her house on his way home but couldn't bring himself to get out of the car. Instead, he just sat there with the engine ticking over for about five minutes before driving away. He knew she'd ask him all the same questions as Lydia—how was he coping, was he still seeing a therapist, would he visit his father's grave on the anniversary, did he know how hard it was for her, even after all these years? He was sure Lydia and his mother were conspiring against him because they saw him as the real reason why his father died that day. That's why they wanted him to see a therapist so that they could drag it out of him. But he could see what they were up to and wasn't going to play into their hands.

When he got home, his neighbour was standing at the top of the stairs again with a pile of posts in her hands, which she'd collected from the mailbox downstairs. She passed him the ones with his name on. He thanked her and took them inside, where he sat down on the couch and began shuffling through them. There were a few utility bills, flyers from local takeaways, a bank statement, and something else.

At the bottom of the pile was an envelope with the words— 'To Eliot Foster'—crudely written on the front of it in large, wobbly letters with big gaps between them.

He turned it over and used his car key to tear it open. Inside was a letter which read:

Dear Eliot,

Do you remember me?

I'm the one who was there when Dad hit his head, the one who sleeps beside you in bed.

I tried to visit, but you weren't home; perhaps next time, I'll try the phone.

Or maybe I'll see Lydia first, that girl sure has a terrible thirst for bad little boys who hide their toys where not even they can find them.

From an old friend

First, he felt confusion, then paranoia, and finally, rage. *How dare they,* he thought, pacing back and forth. He was sure this was the work of Lydia's secret lover. She must have told them about the car crash while she was bitching about how he couldn't just get over it, even after years of therapy. And how he still had night terrors about seeing his father's head go through the windscreen.

She doesn't get it; she'll never get it, he thought. All her life, her parents had sheltered her from harm, while his parents had put him directly in its path when he was just a kid, barely old enough to understand the world around him.

He decided to drive to Lydia's house. *Maybe I'll catch her in the act,* he thought—half fearful, half hopeful he'd find her in the arms of another. At least then, he'd know. At least then, the whirring in his brain would stop.

It was dark when he pulled into the driveway of Lydia's family home. The curtains were drawn, but the lights were on inside. He got out of the car, slamming the door behind him. Then he walked up to the front door and pounded on it three times with his fist clenched.

"I know you're in there; you can't hide. Come out and face me!" he shouted, stepping back and looking up at the house.

A woman's face appeared in one of the downstairs windows, from behind the curtain. It was Lydia's mother. Eliot had only met her a couple of times during the two years he and Lydia had been dating, but he recognized the wide-eyed expression she wore—he'd seen it many times on a younger version of the same face.

The face disappeared. Angered, he began chanting, "Come out, come out, wherever you are." Then the lights in the house went out.

It suddenly occurred to him that perhaps Lydia was at his mother's house. *Maybe it was Mum who wrote the letter,* he thought. He got back in the car and sped backwards out of the driveway, the tires screeching as he revved the engine.

Something glimmered in his rearview mirror, but before he could hit the brakes, a muffled thud came from the back of the car. He froze, his hands gripping the steering wheel, his eyes cast downward. He daren't look.

It was only when Lydia's mother came out of the house and screamed as she saw her daughter's body underneath his car, that he realised the horror of what he'd done.

Madame V

She looked nothing like anyone he'd ever seen before. To most, that might sound like a cliché, but in this case, it was true. When she swept into the room in her flowing black skirt, purple blouse, and with long, dark hair, he knew he had to speak to her.

He was just a baby-faced student, hanging out at a house party with friends. But he caught her eye, and with a mischievous look on her face, she offered to read his palm if he got her a drink.

She held his hand in hers, admiring his long, slender fingers before gently tracing the creases of his palm with her fingertips. "You're going to buy a blue car," she said.

She must be a fake, he thought, because he didn't even have a driving license yet, let alone the inclination to buy a new car.

"You're going to get a new job," she continued.

He again doubted her legitimacy, because he was a full-time student, the only job he could manage was working a couple of night shifts at a bar in town, collecting glasses. And the one he had suited him just fine, though he did fall asleep in lectures sometimes after working into the early hours of the morning.

"And I see a woman in your future," she said.

"A woman?" he asked.

"Yes. Does that surprise you?"

"It's just that, I'm not really looking for anything right now," he said coyly, thinking that this was her way of flirting with him.

"Ah, but that doesn't mean it's not looking for you." She winked and sipped from her glass before taking a seat in the corner of the crowded room.

He looked around, realising that his friends had dispersed, probably in search of girls and alcohol. So, he followed her, eager to know more about this strange woman who had crossed his path.

He asked her name and what other things she'd seen with her gift. She went by V and had been seeing spirits since she was thirteen. She'd seen medieval monks and Victorian orphans, received phone calls from beyond the grave, foretold her best friend's death, and been visited by a dead ex-lover.

As tall as these tales were, he felt compelled to keep talking to her. There was something about her manner of speaking—the way she moved her hands and made the most ordinary things sound poetic—that was mesmerising.

She was a gypsy and a witch, from the silk scarf in her hair to the velvet crescent moon slippers she wore on her feet. Every garment she wore seemed to tell a story of its own.

When the party ended, his friends went into town with a few other guests, while the two of them headed back to his bedsit.

The next morning, he brought her breakfast in bed. As the morning light filtered through the curtains, he noticed that she was quite a bit older than him. Deep laughter lines framed either side of her mouth, and her hair was greying. She looked as though she'd led a whole life before him, though it was clear they'd led very different lives. She told him she was always travelling and hadn't seen her family in years. She'd been to India and Egypt more than once, while the furthest he'd travelled was Cornwall with his family.

What could a woman as worldly as she possibly want with a geek like him, he wondered.

"You're a Pisces, aren't you?" she asked, sipping her coffee. "I can tell."

"So they tell me. Though, I've never really bought into all that rubbish," he said.

"Oh, me neither," she said. "I'd be a cynic if it weren't for this second sight of mine."

Somehow he found that hard to believe. It was true that, despite her elaborate clothing, she had a down-to-earth quality about her. She swore like a sailor and told it like it was. But still, she earned a living telling fortunes and talked to spirits at bus stops.

She told him that she'd be at the arts bar on campus one night later that week, and that he should stop by if he found the time.

After she'd finished her coffee, she went into the bathroom and came out ten minutes later wearing the clothes she'd had on the night before, with black kohl eyeliner and blue shadow painted on her eyes, like a sarcophagus mask.

He got dressed and went to a university tutorial later that morning, on an English poet who was known for his straightforward and at times, darkly humorous way of writing about the world. Now there was a cynic, he thought. Or perhaps he was an optimist, disillusioned by reality. He wondered if that was what was slowly happening to him, and whether he had chosen to study literature to find out if anyone else had ever felt the same way about the world as he did.

V was well-read, evident in the way she seamlessly wove phrases and analogies from both classic and lesser-known works into her speech. But whenever she referenced. Whenever she referenced these works, he felt as though she truly grasped their deeper meaning, as if she had lived them herself.

On his way to the arts bar that Thursday evening, he visited a small, independent bookseller and purchased a book about spiritual connections. The night they'd met, she'd affectionately called him her "soul friend." So, on the inside cover, he wrote: "To V, from a soul friend."

She was speaking emphatically to a young couple about the healing and restorative powers of the colour blue when he entered the bar.

"The Native Americans believed turquoise to be a tremendously powerful stone, with the ability to heal and soothe

the sick," she went on. Her many bangles clinked together as she moved her arms. It was like watching a theatrical performance.

He ordered a pint of beer for himself and waited for her to finish. Then, when the couple had thanked her for her wisdom and gone on their way, she turned, pretending to be surprised to see him.

"Glad you could make it," she said. "But I can't stay long; I have a train to catch."

"Can I get you a drink?" he asked.

"Ooh, yes, please. I'll have another glass of red," she said, winking at the barman.

He thought, from her slow, exaggerated movements, that she'd probably already had quite a few drinks before he'd arrived. But it was the polite thing to do, and he'd walk her to the train station to make sure she got on safely.

They took a booth, and he noticed that she seemed melancholic compared to the almost manic character he'd met at the house party. She was slumped in her seat, looking down into her drink, muttering about how she had no choice and how she'd longed to be an artist, but sometimes life has other ideas. He could barely get a word in edgewise to ask her what she meant before she asked him for the time and said she'd have to be going.

They walked and talked until they reached the station. Just before the train was due to arrive, he handed her the book he'd bought. She recognised the author immediately and embraced him after reading the inscription.

"Bless you," she said, stroking his cheek with the back of her hand.

"Where do you live?" he asked. "Perhaps I could visit sometime."

"Oh, you don't have to do that."

"But what if I wanted to?" he asked, thinking she was only being polite.

Her train arrived before she could give him a proper answer, so he wished her goodbye and a safe journey, telling her that he'd see her again soon. She didn't say anything more and waved to him as the train doors closed behind her.

Two weeks passed without a word. He went to the arts bar a few times but never saw her there. Without her full name, the only thing he knew was that she'd ended up at the same house party as him, meaning she must have known someone else there. Though he couldn't recall seeing her with anyone else that night. He asked the people who rented the house if they knew of a bohemian woman who was a clairvoyant, but they didn't. Then just when he was starting to lose hope of ever finding her, he overheard a conversation between two course mates, with the girl saying that she'd visited a fortune teller at a travelling fair that was in town.

He managed to convince a couple of his friends to go to the fair with him, though they didn't know the real reason he wanted to go. He hadn't told anyone about his liaisons with V. If he was honest with himself, it was because he felt ashamed that, instead of dating a girl his own age, he was chasing one almost twice his age—someone he didn't really know at all, and who seemed to have a drinking problem, among other vices. Perhaps there was something in her that he was missing, or maybe he was just bored and needed someone to fix in order to make his own life seem more interesting. It was like a compulsion. He had to see her and speak to her again.

The fair comprised a few suspicious-looking wagons, a carousel, a ghost train, spinning teacups, a hall of mirrors, and several smaller stalls with large, hand-painted signs showing the names of the acts inside. There was a puppet show, with two marionettes fighting over a third, dressed in a bridal gown, while a group of children laughed and pointed. There was Periwinkle the clown, making odd balloon creatures, surrounded by a crowd of children and their disquieted parents. Then there was Farizaar, the fire breather, whose audience seemed both fascinated and terrified. And finally, there was Madame V, the fortune teller, who knew your destiny and had gained expertise in palmistry and tarot while travelling to exotic lands around the world.

He headed towards Madame V's stall and paid the man holding the black curtain that covered the entrance. He was a tall man in his mid-to-late-forties, with a dark complexion and an accent that seemed to be a blend of many places. Beyond the curtain, though the lighting was dim, he could see that the inside of the stall had been arranged to resemble a Victorian parlour, with red flocked wallpaper, gas lamps, and a dresser cluttered with animal skulls, glass bottles containing brightly coloured, mysterious substances, and a taxidermied raven. At the centre, was a circular table draped in cloth, and sitting at it was a woman with her hands on a crystal ball. As he moved closer, he noticed that she wore a black lace veil over her head, obscuring her face.

"Take a seat, darling," she said in a familiar voice.

He sat down and strained his eyes, trying to see the face behind the veil.

"You're looking for someone," she said.

"I'm looking for a woman," he replied wearily. "I'd hoped she'd be here, but it seems I've had a wasted journey."

"What makes you think that?"

"Because the woman I know doesn't believe in all this rubbish," he said, gesturing to the numerous props around the room.

"Let me guess, she's a cynic?"

"Yes."

"But she's been on this earth a lot longer than you and has seen many more things to be cynical about."

"How would you know what I have to be cynical about?" he asked, standing up. "There's you, for one."

"All of this is for show, but not the messages. No, they're from spirits."

He sat back down.

"And that man outside, I suppose he's part of the show, too?"

She sighed and drew the veil back from her face. "Well, I didn't tell you the whole truth. I'm married and I have a daughter. But you must understand—what I told you that night is real. There is a woman in your future. You were just mistaken in thinking it was me."

"Then why did you come into my life?"

"Because you came into mine. It's been a long time since someone has looked at me the way you did and listened to me. And I mean *really* listened."

He could think of no worthy retort. She'd led him on for her own reasons, but he had wanted to believe.

On reflection, he felt foolish—thinking that this older, married woman, who lived on a travelling fair could offer him the wisdom that her alluring appearance promised. She, like him, was lost, but in her own unique way. She didn't have the answers. But perhaps she was part of it—someone he was meant to meet along the way. Before he left the stall, she handed him back the book he had given her. He opened the cover and read his own handwriting:

'To V, from a soul friend.'

"One more thing I wanted to ask," he said, on his way out. "What's your name?"

"Vivienne," she said.

"It's nice, you should use it more often," he said, lifting the curtain to see the bright green grass and colourful fair rides beyond it.

She gave a bittersweet smile and wished him luck for the future as he left.

He found his friends watching the fire-breather in amazement while stuffing their faces with candy floss.

"Where've you been?" one of them asked.

"Oh, just catching up with an old friend," he said. "Should we get out of here?"

Having no use for the book he bought for Vivienne, he dropped it off at a second hand shop on the way home.

A few months later, he was taking driving lessons in the blue banger that his uncle had sold to him for next to nothing when he saw a familiar figure leaving one of the blocks of flats in a rundown part of town. She was wearing a brown suede coat and blue jeans, and her long, dark hair was hanging in a single plait down her back. And with her was a girl of about ten or twelve years of age, with the same face as her mother. He watched as the two of them walked down the street in the opposite direction. It was sobering to see her in this light—as a stranger, as a mother. She'd led a whole life before him.

He drove home and then headed to work. His shifts at the bar were beginning to affect his studies, but he'd managed to find a part-time position at the café in the student guild. It was only two days a week, but it topped up his student loan, and he enjoyed the atmosphere.

While he was cleaning tables, he saw that there was a girl sitting by the window, reading a book he recognised. He went over to her and noticed she looked quite engrossed in it, with her feet up on the other chair at the table and two empty cups beside her.

"Looks interesting," he said, gesturing to the book, smiling.

She looked up, a smirk on her face. "It is, actually. Bought it today. Says, 'To V from a soul friend' on the inside. I wonder who it belonged to before me."

"I wonder," he said. "Don't you love the way second hand books tell a story?"

Bones and Trinkets

Crowe's Undertakers was a small, discreet business on the corner of a Victorian terrace. It had a black front door with a bell above it, a window, and a hand-painted sign showing the name of the family that had run it for generations.

Victor Crowe was the latest in a long line of proprietors who charged a modest fee to appeal to those in desperate need of his services. He was shrewd, methodical, and formal in his manner. Any who did business with him could expect a firm handshake but no sympathy for their loss. Yet he was never short of custom because there were always deaths, and his prices were all that some could afford.

However, despite his outward professionalism, Crowe was hiding a grave secret. All his life, he'd been an avid collector—as a boy, it was insects and small animals he could preserve in a jar or matchbox.

Yet, as an adult, he had developed an appetite for rarer treasures: hearts, fingers, eyeballs, and teeth. He didn't know where his fascination with these items came from or when exactly it had started. Perhaps it was inherited. His father had been a medically minded man, and Crowe had a lucid memory of a time when his father had shown him a foetus in a jar—the umbilical cord still attached—though he couldn't remember whether his collecting had started before or after that day.

Over the years, he'd amassed quite the collection, which he kept stored under lock and key in the basement of the funeral home, where the deceased waited until he prepared them for burial—using makeup and clothing to cleverly disguise any unsightly stitches or missing appendages. To the untrained eye, Crowe's funeral home was just like any other—grey and dreary, except for a few unusual items arranged on his desk and the shelves behind it. Among these objects was a beetle forever frozen in a glass paperweight, a raven's skull, an hourglass filled with black sand, some taxidermied moths under a glass cloche, and a selection of old anatomical charts.

Crowe worked alone, so there was never anyone to challenge his methods. That was, at least, until Lavinia Blackwood arrived on his doorstep one fateful morning.

It was eight o'clock, and Crowe had barely finished unlocking the door and opening the curtains when a well-dressed lady in her late seventies or eighties walked in. The bell over the door chimed sharply, announcing her arrival, as though it were of utmost importance that he look up from his desk and greet her that very instant.

"Morning," he said sombrely, still wiping the remnants of his breakfast from his lips.

"Good morning, sir. I've come to enquire about funeral arrangements," she said, already unbuttoning her fur coat and sitting in the chair across from him.

"Then you've come to the right place. Whose funeral is it, may I ask?" he said, taking a pen and some paper to jot down the details.

"Mine. Well, not yet, of course, but soon, I should think."

She said this so matter-of-factly that he looked up from the paper, taken aback. Most of the people who came through his door were snivelling wrecks with tissues held to their noses—but not her. The composure with which she had told him something so momentous was astounding, even by his own standards.

"Though, I must warn you, my preferences are very particular. I would like to be embalmed and to be wearing my favourite red dress with my emerald necklace and matching earrings for my burial. Which brings me to my final request—the burial must take place within a day or two of my death, no later."

"I see," he said, eyebrows furrowed. "The thing is, M—"

"Blackwood. Mrs. Lavinia Blackwood," she asserted.

"Mrs. Blackwood... the thing is, I typically need at least a week to ensure the body is ready for viewings from friends and family."

"I have no friends or family left," she said, a sorrowful look in her eyes. "Mr. Crowe, I beg you to make an exception."

"Mrs. Blackwood, I really must—"

"I will pay double your fee," she interrupted.

Now, she had captured his interest.

It was clear from her way of dress and generous offer that money was of no concern to her. Then why, he wondered, had she chosen the undertaker with the lowest fee for miles around? As if hearing his thoughts aloud, she answered.

"I suppose you're wondering why I chose this funeral home and not, say, Serene Shores in the town. Well, you see, I wanted the personal touch. My late husband was a renowned surgeon and always spoke so highly of the funerals you conducted for his... less fortunate patients."

Crowe searched his memory for an elderly gentleman by the name of Blackwood but could think of no one. He'd had many acquaintances throughout his career, not all of whom were burying loved ones—some were instead profiting from others' losses.

One such acquaintance was a man named Cecil, who had purchased several specimens from Crowe over the years, including corneas, a kidney, a small intestine, and, rather curiously, a tongue. They had met several times throughout Victor's career, which he'd embarked on at the tender age of eighteen and remained devoted to well into his sixties.

In spite of their loyalty to one another as business partners, however, Crowe had never learned Cecil's surname. Yet he was such a vibrant and colourful character that a second name would have seemed redundant. And so Crowe knew him only as the eccentric with a morbid curiosity about human anatomy and more money than he knew what to do with. Just a man with an unusual hobby who had inherited a small fortune, which he used to purchase macabre trinkets.

Indeed, the only reason Crowe was able to offer such competitive prices was that he had other means of making money. As rare a creature as he was in his habits, he was not alone, for there were others who shared his perverse interests. There was a niche crowd willing to pay a handsome sum for an organ that was still quite fresh and not yet emitting a foul odour, or for a delectable morsel of viscera pickled in a glass jar.

"I'm sorry to hear about your husband's passing," he told her.

"He was taken from me last winter, God rest his soul," she said, drawing a cross in the air. "It was that damned blood transfusion that did it. Science isn't always right."

There was clearly more to the story of Mr. Blackwood's tragic demise, but Crowe didn't wish to press the matter, so he instead began to go through the funeral arrangements with her, taking note of any specific requests. She would be embalmed, dressed, sealed inside the coffin, and interred in a family grave shortly thereafter.

Once they had agreed on the particulars and she had paid him, they bid each other a good day.

As she opened the door, the bell tinkling over her head, she said, "I trust you'll do as I ask."

To which he replied, "You have my word."

She smiled and left, pulling the door shut behind her.

A week later, she was dead.

The call came from the hospital mortuary, which arranged for the body to be transported to Crowe's funeral home, where it was carefully lifted down the stairs to the basement and laid upon a ceramic slab. There, Crowe swiftly went to work, assessing the appearance of the recently deceased.

Lavinia Blackwood seemed to have died peacefully, with a serene smile on her face. Her eyes were closed, her hair hung in silver ringlets around her face, and in a plastic bag beside her were the clothes she'd asked to be dressed in.

Following the same routine he had for many years, Crowe laid the tools of his trade out on a metal trolley and began cleaning the body, before putting caps over the eyes and stitching the mouth shut. Then, with a scalpel, he made a small incision by the collarbone and fed a tube into the carotid artery to let the blood drain from the body, while a machine pumped embalming fluid through it.

When it came to opening the cavity, however, Crowe paused, thinking back to the last thing Lavinia said to him on her way out the door— "I trust you'll do as I ask."

It was that word—"trust." He'd heard it many times before in his line of work from mourning family members. They trusted him to take care of their loved ones, and they trusted him not to sell their precious heirlooms and the body parts of their nearest and dearest to his unscrupulous business associates. What fools, he thought. By placing their trust in him, the families relinquished any control over what happened to their loved ones the moment they descended into his basement.

Without any next of kin, Lavinia Blackwood was no different from the rest of the unfortunate souls who had passed through his hands.

Using a scalpel and rib cutter, Crowe opened the cavity, revealing the internal organs. But to his utter astonishment, the heart he found there was not that of an elderly woman. The tissue was soft, lean, and vivid with life. Lavinia's words—"I trust you'll do as I ask"—echoed through his mind once more as he admired the heart in his hands. Crimson with the very essence of vitality, it was almost hypnotic and seemed to whisper to him softly from somewhere deep within its chambers. He would close the cavity but keep the heart for himself.

It was perhaps the rarest treasure he'd found yet while delving into the corpses of those unlucky enough to fall into his care, and he was not about to let it slip through his fingers. Carefully, he wrapped it and put it in the refrigerator to keep it fresh until he knew what he was going to do with it.

Once he'd finished sewing the cavity in Lavinia's body, he dressed her, put on her jewellery, and applied makeup to her face and neck, bringing colour back to her complexion.

He then painted her fingernails with red polish before folding her hands, one over the other, as he had done so many times before. In the days before her burial, he kept her body in the backroom of the funeral home. He hadn't sealed the coffin, but he wasn't expecting her to have any visitors.

The only people Crowe was expecting to see were a couple of his villainous business partners—Horace and Maguire—who had agreed to purchase her jewellery. After all, it seemed a shame to bury it, considering its obvious value.

The following afternoon, while sitting at his desk, Crowe noticed a man standing on the opposite side of the street. He was an older man, short and portly, with a grey beard, dressed in black.

At first, Crowe thought he might have been waiting for someone, but then he saw the man was looking directly at him, and had begun crossing the street. Crowe quickly took some papers from a drawer under his desk and started shuffling them, to make himself look busy. The bell above the door chimed as the man entered and stood at Crowe's desk.

"Afternoon, Sir. How can I be of service?" Crowe asked, looking up with a smile.

"I've come to see Lavinia Blackwood," the bearded man said, his voice carrying an Irish lilt. Perturbed, Crowe fumbled in his desk drawer once more, this time searching for Lavinia's file.

"You'll have to excuse me, I can't see that my client was expecting any visitors," Crowe said, trying to maintain his composure.

"Perhaps not, yet here I am," the man responded, his tone assertive, leaving Crowe unsure of how to proceed.

"Run this place alone, do you?" the man asked, now examining the display of items on the shelves. He turned over the hourglass, watching as the black sand began to gather in a small heap.

"Just me," Crowe said, glancing behind him as if checking for a secret assistant. "Sorry, I don't think I got your name."

"It's Fallow. I'm an old, old friend of Lavinia's and her husband."

The repetition of 'old' struck Crowe as odd. While his unwelcome visitor was advancing in years, he maintained a certain vigour—both of body and mind—that betrayed his age.

"You wouldn't mind if I spent a moment alone with her, would you? We have unfinished business," Fallow said, his hand already on the handle of the door to the backroom.

His forcefulness angered Crowe, though he had to admit he felt an inclination from somewhere deep within to follow his lead as if an invisible string joined them. All these years, Crowe had guarded a secret, like a bird guarding its nest, and here was a man who could ruin it all by opening doors that ought to stay closed.

"Of course, but please do be careful, she is in a rather delicate condition," Crowe said, rushing to meet him at the door.

As they went through to the backroom, a cold air swept over them. Lavinia lay silently in her casket, lined with red velvet, as though she were only sleeping.

"Hello, my darling," said Fallow, leaning in to kiss her gently on the forehead. "I'd like a moment alone with her, please, if that's alright with you," he continued, his face still next to hers.

"Of course, I'll just be in the other room," Crowe said, reluctantly stepping out. He closed the door behind him, leaving it slightly ajar, and hovered just outside, listening to what was happening on the other side. He could hear Fallow whispering in his deep, gruff voice but couldn't make out the words.

A few minutes later, Fallow came out. "You've done a grand job; if I didn't know any better, I'd say she was only sleeping," he told Crowe as if commenting on the quality of his work.

"I try my best," Crowe replied, maintaining his calm exterior.

"It's just... I couldn't help but notice there's something missing," Fallow added, his eyes fixed on Crowe.

"Well, there's only so much you can do to get the likeness," Crowe muttered, unsure of where this was leading.

"Indeed," Fallow said. His eyes never wavered from Crowe, sending a chill down his spine. With one final glance, he turned and left, briefly looking back through the window before continuing on his way.

Lavinia's burial was only a couple of days away, but sensing Fallow knew something he didn't, Crowe was eager to seal the coffin. He couldn't risk anyone else seeing the body, especially not with the mysterious aura surrounding it.

Before sealing it, he removed her jewellery and placed it in the safe behind the cabinets of chemical vials along the back wall of the basement.

When the body was first brought to the funeral home, Crowe had been given a bag of her belongings, which contained the clothes she wanted to be dressed in for her burial, her jewellery, and a handbag with a purse inside it. He opened the purse—inside were a few coins, some receipts, a boiled sweet, and a small photograph. It appeared to be from a wedding congregation standing on the steps of a church. Holding it closer, he could see the bride was Lavinia, perhaps in her thirties. To her right was a youthful Fallow, and to her left stood the groom, who looked strangely familiar.

Bringing the photograph closer to his face, Crowe was hit with the sudden realization that the man standing beside Lavinia was none other than his old business associate, Cecil. This realization was swiftly followed by several others, each one more alarming than the last. The first was that Lavinia had almost certainly been aware of her husband's crooked dealings with him; the second was that Fallow was also aware of them; and the third was that the three friends had profited from these dealings in ways that were still unknown to him.

He thought of Lavinia's certainty that death was near on the day she'd visited the funeral home and how she wanted a quick burial. What was she hiding? And of all people, why did she trust me to keep it a secret? he wondered. Where, or who, did the heart come from?

Needing to know more, Crowe went to retrieve Lavinia's file from his desk drawer. In it, he found the papers she'd signed on the day she visited the funeral home, along with some medical papers from the coroner, including the death certificate.

To his surprise, she had lived in a rundown part of town in a Victorian building that had been converted into flats. He had passed it many times and couldn't imagine her, in her luxurious attire, sharing close quarters with the waifs and strays he often saw lingering on the steps of the ramshackle building. If she and her husband were so well off, then why had she spent her last days in poverty? He asked himself, bewildered.

Turning to her medical papers, he saw that a toxicology report had confirmed the presence of drugs in her system. An enormous quantity of sleeping pills, which were prescribed to her for insomnia, had been taken several hours prior to her being discovered by a neighbour. She was pronounced dead at the scene. Crowe looked at the death certificate and read: "Cause of death: suicide by overdose."

Suddenly, it became clear why she had been so certain of her own death just days before it occurred. But the more he learned about Lavinia Blackwood, the more she eluded him. His interest in her was unique in the sense that he had never given a second thought about the backstories of any of those from whom he salvaged treasures.

And most importantly, his interest in her was inextricably bound to the secret life he had led for the past four decades. Finding the key to her secret meant finding the key to his own— the true reason these three friends were involved with him.

The following day, he took the bus to Nightingale Heights, where Lavinia had spent her final years, seemingly estranged from her husband. The man living in the flat across from her told Crowe she had lived there for about nine years and that he always saw her alone. She never had any visitors and kept to herself, except for the odd trip to the post office or corner shop. Occasionally, he would bring her a newspaper or a bottle of milk, but he didn't profess to know her well.

Crowe told the building manager he was Lavinia's son and had come to collect his late mother's belongings. In his experience, death had a way of stopping the questions you might ordinarily receive in these sorts of situations. He was a stranger, and yet there he was, unlocking the door to this woman's flat.

Inside, there was an overwhelming stench of dampness, which was visibly soaking through the wallpaper underneath the long, rectangular window in the living room. In there, was just a chair, a TV, and a small folding table, which he imagined she ate her dinners on.

Off the living room were a kitchen, a bedroom, and a bathroom, all still decorated in styles from thirty to forty years earlier. He went into the bedroom, where he pulled out three cardboard boxes from under the bed, which were filled with papers, photographs, and newspaper clippings.

Rummaging through one of them, he found photographs of Lavinia, Cecil, and a girl who looked slightly older in each one. There were pictures of family holidays, her first day of school, her last day of school, prom, starting university—and then, nothing.

Among these were letters addressed to Lavinia from someone named Seamus. But there was one letter in her handwriting. It was dated April 6th—the day she died. She had written it and then chosen not to send it for some reason. Picking it up, Crowe read:

Dear Seamus,

It is with a heavy heart that I write to inform you of Cecil's passing last Winter. He was a loving husband to me, a devoted father to our daughter Delara, and a loyal friend to you.

In recent years, we have been distant from one another with all that has happened. Though I know I don't need to remind you and that we both find it too painful to speak of, even after all these years.

It will be my time to go soon, and I want the past to be buried with me. I believe that our daughter was taken to punish us for our sins against others, and I have carried the guilt like a heavy stone for so long that I can bear its weight no longer.

I will take our secret to the grave in the hopes that I can atone for the hurt we caused. In time, I pray you will find peace and learn to let go, as I have done. Until then, I will wait for you on the other side with our beloved Delara.

Love always, Lavinia.

Her neighbour had been right—she and her husband, Cecil, had become estranged. They had been driven apart by the death of their daughter and perhaps something else. This was a goodbye letter, a suicide note, to someone she loved—tender and filled with sorrow.

He delved into the box once more, this time finding a newspaper clipping from thirty years earlier. The photograph was of the girl in the family pictures, and the title of the article was: 'Student Tragically Killed by Drunk Driver.'

Skim reading it, he discovered that Lavinia's eighteen-year-old daughter was walking back to her dorm one night when she was run down by a drunk driver who fled the scene and crashed the car just a couple of miles outside the university campus. They had survived, escaping with only minor injuries, but she had slipped into a coma and died four days later in hospital. Her organs were donated to save the lives of five other people.

Crowe thought about the young heart he had removed from Lavinia's body—was it possible she took her daughter's heart? he wondered. He continued reading and came across the words:

'The success of the transplants was due to the masterful work of consultant surgeons, Mr Hartwell and Mr Fallow. The former of the two, who is the victim's father, said he believes that it's possible to find good in even the worst of circumstances.'

The pieces began falling into place for Crowe. Lavinia's husband and Fallow had worked together, not just as medical professionals, but as con men who had used their positions to facilitate a covert operation. Was this what she meant by 'sins' in her letter? Crowe thought to himself. After all, she must have known about her husband's private dealings with him, and she had been a beneficiary of their work by receiving the heart of someone a mere fraction of her age.

But some questions remained unanswered. Who was Seamus, and what part did he have to play in all this? Did the heart really belong to her daughter? And with the other two now dead, why was Fallow hanging around like a bad smell?

In the days following his first visit, Crowe had seen Fallow outside the funeral home many times. His movements followed no discernible pattern—they could happen at any time, day or night. He would stop across the street or in front of the window and just stare with his piercing blue eyes as if searching for something.

Meanwhile, Crowe was becoming increasingly anxious about the heart in his basement. Since putting it there, he'd barely slept a wink—grabbing an hour here and an hour there, wherever he could. A couple of times, he'd nodded off at his desk and woken up to find Fallow lurking on his doorstep like a bad omen.

Sometimes at night, after he'd locked up and gone to bed, he thought he heard the heart beating. Though he knew this could only be his mind playing tricks, it still terrified him. Yet, he could not bring himself to destroy it or put it back where he found it.

He had considered both those options, but something about it was so alluring that he couldn't bear to part with it. To him, it was more than flesh; it was the culmination of his life's work and symbolic of life itself. To let it go would be to accept the end, to embrace death.

All the years he'd spent collecting body parts and preserving them, he thought he was saving them from rot and decay. Once they were put in the earth and covered with soil, time took them back with its withered hands and crushed them into dust. He saw it as a sacrilege and a waste for something so beautiful to be erased. But, surrounded by the eternal vitality of his collection, he felt he could cheat death.

The morning of Lavinia's burial, Crowe rose early and went to the graveyard to see the plot where she was to be interred. It was secluded under an old yew tree, with the statue of a sleeping angel on top of the white marble tombstone. Engraved on the front of the stone, in gold writing, were the words:

'In loving memory of Delara Maryam Hartwell, beloved daughter, 23.05.1976 - 06.04.1994. William Cecil Hartwell, devoted husband and father, 09.12.1944 - 27.11.2023. Lavinia Pearl Blackwood, loving wife and mother, 14.06.1946 - 06.04.2024.'

"Nice spot, isn't it?" a familiar voice said. Crowe turned to see Fallow emerging from behind the thick, dark trunk of the yew tree.

"It's quite lovely," Crowe said, unnerved to see his pursuer.

"It should never have happened," said Fallow, now standing beside Crowe, the pair of them looking at the tombstone. It was unclear which tragedy he was referring to since there were two people already in the grave, with a third waiting to join them.

"She never told me they had a daughter," Crowe said, hoping to break the tense silence between them because it made him nervous.

"Well, he didn't, though he never knew it. Lavinia swore me to secrecy. Said it'd break his heart if he found out. But of course, it wasn't his heart but hers that broke the day Delara died."

Hearing this, Crowe realised he was standing next to the man from Lavinia's letters—Seamus Fallow. His Irish lilt, the way he'd called her 'my darling' the day he came to visit, his friendship with her husband, his face in the wedding photograph—it all made sense. Delara was his daughter, not Cecil's.

Out of the corner of his eye, Crowe could see tears rolling down his counterpart's face. "I'm sorry for your loss," he said.

"She couldn't let her go. Said she wanted to carry a piece of her, always. She promised that as long as she lived, so too would Delara. So, I gave it to her. But look at her now—dead and by her own hand." As he said this, a fierceness came out in his voice, almost like the growl of a frightened and wounded animal.

"I know you have the heart, Crowe, and I need it back," he went on.

Fearing what he might do next, Crowe stepped onto the other side of the open burial plot, away from Fallow.

"I don't know what you're talking about," he said.

"Yes, you do. I've been watching you for almost forty years, picking apart the bodies we sent you like a bird pecking at roadkill. We let you turn a profit because it kept you sweet. Now, do you really think I wouldn't notice you stealing my daughter's heart for your precious collection?"

Speechless after what he'd just heard, Crowe stared, mouth agape, at Fallow, who was glowering at him.

What does he mean— 'the bodies we sent you'? Crowe thought. It suddenly dawned on him that the majority of his clients had been young and in good health, either killed by suicide or in other unfortunate circumstances, such as car accidents. Though it had always struck him as odd that there seemed to be an inordinate number of tragic events happening in one place, he hadn't questioned it, instead choosing to view it as an advantage for his own ends. But now, he felt like a complete fool, used as nothing more than a pawn in an elaborate scheme.

"Why me?" asked Crowe.

"Why? Because you were an easy target. You were so sure of your own control when really your obsession with the preservation of life and immortality was born out of your fear of death. It was all too easy to pull the strings and make you dance," said Fallow, a cruel smirk on his lips.

"And what makes you any different?"

"You know, when I first started out as a surgeon, I really wanted to push the boundaries of science. I truly believed it was possible to cheat death."

"So what changed?"

Fallow was silent, his eyes cast towards the tombstone.

"Her." he began sobbing, then lunged at Crowe, grabbing him by the shoulders. "Give it back! It doesn't belong to you, it belongs to me!"

They were now standing over the hole in the ground like an arch, each holding the other. Fallow was the stronger and larger-framed of the two, but as he felt Crowe's hands grip his throat, his legs buckled.

They struggled, pushing each other back and forth, hovering precariously on the edges of the pit. Fallow began to turn purple in the face as Crowe tightened his grip. Then as the two locked eyes, the colour suddenly drained from Fallow's face and he collapsed, falling face down into the pit. His body hit the coffins of Cecil and Delara below with a final, sickening thud. Having almost fallen into the pit himself, Crowe stumbled, regained his balance, and peered down into the darkness at the lifeless body of his tormentor below.

After a few seconds, the reality of what had just happened began to set in. The thick morning fog now felt as if it was suffocating him as he gasped for air, a cold sweat breaking across his forehead, his hands trembling. The graveyard seemed to be closing in around him, while the pit at his feet seemed to be deepening.

For all his work with the dead, for all his efforts to master his knowledge of the thing he feared most, he realised that death was never the enemy. The real enemy was the terror of facing it and knowing that, one day, it would claim him too.

113

The Witch of the Cave

Halbrook was a small mining town near the coast that had made a name for itself by trading sandstone from the quarry on which it was built.

Nora Moss had spent her whole life there. She was fifteen and had been invited to her first party. It was Halloween, and the rest of her classmates had planned to meet on The Heaps by the old quarry, where they'd drink stolen alcohol and smoke their parents' cigarettes. Or worse. The Heaps were a group of steep, sandy mounds made up of all the waste produced by the quarry. And they were the chosen venue of many of the teenage gatherings that took place in the town.

Below The Heaps was the cave, which had a series of dank, narrow tunnels that ran deep into the cliff on the town's coastline. They were the original mining shafts but had since been abandoned and become the subject of superstition. Schoolkids said that a witch lived there, after somebody found a dead cat and started a rumour. It was the sort of place where rumours could spread quickly. Nora knew that all too well.

Having endured the past four years at the only high school in the town, she was not known for the things she would have liked to have been known for, or for things that were even true. Although her peers recognised that she was clever and gifted, they would often use those things against her, out of resentment. And so she was known as the weird, quiet girl, who looked different from everyone else. She'd never had a boyfriend, only friends who were boys, which could only mean one thing in their eyes. That she liked girls, they only saw what they wanted to, but it wasn't really her.

But during her final year at the school, Nora had reconciled with a lot of the people who were responsible for saying some of the worst things about her, because she wanted to be accepted by them. Not because she wanted to fit in, but so that they would leave her be.

When she was invited to the party, Nora felt that maybe they finally saw that she wasn't so bad after all, and that maybe she was just one of them. Another kid from Halbrook. So she said yes, and started worrying about her outfit.

"What are you going to wear, Nora?" her mother said. "I've got a black dress in the wardrobe that you can borrow."

Nora was close to her mother. They had different personalities, but she'd always felt comforted by the constancy of her mother's love. No matter what kind of a day she'd had at school, or what the other kids thought of her, she was always the same in her mother's eyes. Perfect.

"I could wear it with some black tights, boots, and... What am I going to do for a hat?"

"I'll see what I can dig out", her mother said.

Sure enough, half an hour or so later, she came back with a black witch's hat that had a purple organza bow and fake spider web on it. It had probably been at the back of a wardrobe or at the bottom of a drawer somewhere since the last time she'd been trick or treating. She wondered if all parents held onto their kid's Halloween costumes for that long.

"Fits you better now than it did then!", her mother said, pushing it down onto Nora's head.

"Well, I guess that's my outfit sorted." She smiled awkwardly whilst looking at herself in the full-length mirror.

"Your dad can give you a lift. Where is it?", her mother said.

"Oh, no, that's okay. I'll walk there", said Nora.

Her mother looked up with a furrowed brow.

"No, really. I'll be fine, it's not far."

"Just exactly where is it, Nora?", her mother asked.

"At Evelyn's house", she lied. Evelyn was the most popular girl in her year, and lived in the next street. Her parents had a huge house, which they needed to house their large brood of children.

Her mother seemed to accept this, but wouldn't let her leave the house without wrapping her in a huge, baggy coat on her way out.

"Mum, I can't wear this, it's massive", said Nora, holding her arms out to demonstrate.

"It'll keep you warm, that's all that matters", she replied, waving her down the garden path.

Once Nora's mum had gone back inside, Nora closed the garden gate and turned left towards The Heaps, which were in the opposite direction of Evelyn's house.

She was making her way down the lane at the back of the school sports field, when she heard a familiar voice call her name.

It was dark out, but as she turned around, she saw Rori, Sam, and Alice, a few paces behind. She stopped to let them catch up.

"Are you going to The Heaps, too?" asked Rori, holding a lit cigarette in his right hand, which he then took a drag from.

"Yeah, that's where the party is, isn't it?", she said, noticing that none of them were wearing Halloween costumes.

"Sure is", he said, standing on his cigarette butt.

"Maybe we can walk there together? There's safety in numbers", said Sam.

"I like your hat", said Alice, smiling and touching the brim of Nora's hat. She had quite an impish look about her, with her upturned nose and pouted mouth, which the moonlight only accentuated.

When they got to The Heaps, the others had made a fire from some rocks and fallen tree branches. Some of the boys were tossing their empty beer bottles into it and cheering as they shattered. And someone had brought a stereo, though the music was barely audible over people's conversations.

"So what have you come as, Nora, the witch of the cave?", Evelyn asked, laughing.

"Uh, I guess so", Nora said, looking up at her hat as if to check that she was still wearing it.

"Show us your pussy!" one of the boys shouted. The group erupted into laughter.

"Yeah, show us where you hid the cat". It was getting harder to discern who was speaking, as her eyes welled up with tears and blurred the flames of the fire with the faces encircling it.

"Show us, show us, show us", they started chanting, before moving down The Heaps towards the cave.

Then she felt a pair of hands take hold of her arms and heard a voice whisper in her ear.

"Come on, Nora, you're not scared, are you?" It was Alice, and Nora could smell the sickly sweet scent of beer on her breath, mixed with cigarette smoke.

When they reached the cave, Alice let go of Nora and pushed her, causing her to fall forwards onto the muddy ground. The others gathered around her and watched, like vultures studying their prey.

"I think I'd like to go home, now", Nora said wearily whilst trying to get up.

Then Rori began to recite the old rhyme that every kid from Halbrook knew like the back of their hand. And some of the others began to join in.

Deep within a shadowed cave,

A witch sits quiet, dark and grave.

She disobeyed and played with fire,

Spelling what her heart desired.

The townsfolk heard and came at night,

A mob of rage, a fearsome sight.

Down The Heaps, she sought escape,

The tunnel's mouth, her only shape.

Into the darkness, her fate was cast.

As the rocks gave way, she breathed her last.

The earth swallowed her body whole,

And spat out her restless, immortal soul.

The group had closed in on Nora, leaving no gaps between them for her to break through. She scrambled on her hands and knees into the gaping, black entrance to the cave, and kept moving forward as fast as she could, her clothes becoming heavier as she dragged them through the puddles that had gathered in the uneven surface of the rock.

Someone had gone in after her. She could hear their footsteps echoing through the tunnel walls as they ran, though it was hard to tell which direction they were coming from. The tunnels were long and meandering, and sometimes joined with each other or just kept on going. And then the footsteps stopped and she heard a boy wailing.

She backed herself into a nook and brought her knees up to her chest, unsure what to do next. She couldn't turn back. Whoever it was could be playing a trick on her and the rest of them might still be waiting at the entrance to the cave. She had to carry on and follow the tunnels to the other side, if she had any hope of escaping.

As you would when navigating a maze, she kept a hand on the left wall as she walked, stooped over slightly, so that she didn't hit her head. There was no light or sound, now. It went on like this for what felt like an eternity, until she heard the sound of wind whistling through an opening in the rock. She was almost there.

Soon, there was light again, as she emerged from the other side of the cave onto a dirt path that ran along the coast. She gulped the damp winter air and began to run.

When she got home, her father pulled her close and wouldn't let her go.

"Oh, thank God", he said, and began to sob.

Her mother was on the phone in another room, and Nora heard her say, "She's home, she's home, thank you officer".

Then she came to join them and the three of them stayed in an embrace until her mother said, "Your knees, Nora, they're red raw".

Nora looked down to see that her knees were badly grazed and weeping blood. It must have happened when she was crawling through the tunnels, though she'd been so frantic she hadn't felt it. Her mother changed her wet clothes and then made her sit while she bathed and dressed the wounds.

"We were out of our minds with worry, Nora. When we heard about what happened to that poor boy, we thought the worst", her mother said.

Hearing this, Nora broke out of her trance. The whole night had felt like a bad dream. Something that had happened to someone else and not her. But those words "poor boy", seemed to rouse her from her slumber.

"Poor boy?" asked Nora.

"Sam Vickers is dead", her mother said. "He went into the cave to find you after a silly game went wrong, and hurt himself badly. They couldn't get him out in time".

Nora started to connect the dots. Sam had been there, with Rori and Alice. He'd walked to The Heaps with them and it must have been him and not Rori whose footsteps she'd heard in the cave. And his cries.

She'd thought they'd all betrayed her that she'd been mistaken to give them a second chance. And she had, but for that one boy who really saw her.

Through Her Eyes

She was one of many who I had followed over the years. But for some reason, she stood out from the others. I can't exactly remember when it started, but I guess it was sometime after Max and I broke up.

I was twenty-four when we met, living with my parents to save on rent, and working a dull office job. Meeting new people since leaving university had been harder than I expected. Most of my friends had either stayed in the city or moved back to where they came from. The only other two people I occasionally spent time with were a couple from high school, but even they were struggling with their own issues. They didn't take too kindly to a third wheel showing up outside their flat, asking them if they wanted to get pizza, while they were dealing with their own relationship problems and barely scraping by to pay rent.

I tried online dating as a last-ditch attempt to meet someone because, as I neared my mid-twenties, with thirty just around the corner, the thought of being single while everyone around me was either getting engaged or having kids filled me with dread. I suppose I'd always been scared of being alone, which was ironic given that I'd been alone for most of my life. And if I'd learned anything from previous relationships, it was that you didn't need to be single to feel alone.

Reluctantly, I created an online dating profile and matched with a guy named Max. He was twenty-six, had dark hair and glasses, and claimed to be six foot two—though it later transpired he was closer to five foot ten. We hit it off quickly, bonding over our shared love of indie films and the fact that we both played musical instruments—he played bass guitar, and I played piano. He taught me the word 'pluviophile' because we both loved the rain. Our favourite colour was olive green, and we were both a little socially awkward. He told me that once, he drank a full pot of Earl Grey without any milk because he was too afraid to ask the waitress for some.

After about a week of messaging, he hesitantly asked me if I'd like to meet up sometime, and I said yes. We met in the city after work, and it was pouring down with rain. "You look lovely," he'd said, complimenting my bright red raincoat as I met him outside the vinyl record shop we'd talked about in our messages.

He was dressed in black, with a baseball cap he said he was wearing to disguise the fact that he needed a haircut.

Then, for the next five hours, we walked and talked with little care for the fact that our hair and clothes were getting soaked. We only went to a burrito bar when we both realised it was past ten and we hadn't eaten yet.

Afterwards, we headed to the train station, and he nervously asked, "Would you want to do this again?" to which I said yes. We exchanged numbers, and he caught his train. Mine wasn't due for another fifteen minutes, so I picked a bench on the empty platform and just sat there, reliving the night in my head.

I had high hopes. That night, when I got home, he messaged that he'd had a "really lovely time", and that "we should definitely do this again". But the day after, his tone changed. Whereas before the date he'd seemed enthusiastic and had responded to messages right away, there were now long gaps between his short replies.

I got that feeling in the pit of my stomach—the one I get whenever I sense something is off. I remember feeling it when I was in primary school and imagining that it was a goldfish swimming around inside me, tickling my insides as it did loop-deloops. The only thing I could think to do was message him more and ask him on a second date, to reassure myself that I hadn't just been imagining how he'd felt about me before.

I had no point of comparison to refer to. The only boyfriends I'd had in the past were guys I met at college or university, who I'd developed relationships with organically over time. They knew what I looked like and what to expect. But Max and I were unknown quantities to one another. All I had to go off were his mixed signals, and whether out of optimism or denial, I chose to see his hesitancy as a reflection of his inexperience, rather than a reflection of my inadequacy.

Over the next three months, we ended up spending most of our weekends together. We went to see six films at the cinema, hiked in the woods, visited a Roman city, ate at two expensive restaurants, kissed in my bedroom while half-heartedly watching a television series, and texted every day. He even met my parents.

The day before our supposed tenth date, he told me his sister was ill and he wouldn't be able to make it. When I suggested we reschedule, he told me he wasn't sure he was ready to date yet. That was the last that I ever heard from him. I was down about the whole thing for several months afterwards. I liked Max a lot.

Beneath the shyness and self-deprecating jokes was a kindred spirit—someone who wanted love and had it to give but was crippled by the fear of abandonment. He'd told me several times that he was unlucky in love. One comment, in particular, has stuck with me ever since: "Everyone leaves."

I carried on with my life, trying to find new ways to meet people. I enrolled in night school and even gave online dating another go, but I was quickly put off after meeting a guy who had a belly button fetish and a murderous hatred for his housemate's unusually high-pitched voice.

This failure only made me think of Max more. I began regularly checking on his social media to see what he was up to. But there wasn't much there—just a few edgy posts written about seven years ago and some family pictures he'd been tagged in.

One of them was of him and his sister on the balcony of a resort that looked somewhere exotic. I lingered on this one for a few minutes one night while I was scrolling in bed. I'd never met his sister, though he'd complained about their fallouts many times while we were dating. He'd said she was petty and childish. But in this picture—cheek to cheek, smiling—I couldn't imagine them ever not getting along. She was classically pretty, with shoulder-length dark hair and striking blue eyes. She looked like the female version of him.

I clicked on her name next to the picture—Sophie Harper—and went to her profile. There were lots of pictures of her with friends at parties, weddings, with her family, with friends from university, and even with her classmates on her last day of high school. I scrolled through all her pictures, as far back as her account would go. I even came across a few more of her and Max, including one where he looked about ten and was wearing a T-shirt with a dragon on it.

By the time I was finished, I could see her face even with my eyes closed. The way her left eyebrow was always slightly raised as if she were smug about something she knew and I didn't. The way her cheeks dimpled when she smiled. The way she did her eye makeup so that they looked large and round, turned up at the edges like a cat's.

She was different from her brother in so many ways. She was fun, gregarious, and outgoing, while he was far more serious and reserved. I imagined what it might have been like if we had met—how we'd get on instantly and how she'd tell Max that it was great he'd finally got a girlfriend who she saw as a sister. I fell asleep with the phone in my hand.

The next morning, while brushing my teeth, I found myself searching her name on the internet to see what else I could learn about her. She was a children's party host and did things like triathlons in her spare time. She travelled a lot and promoted beauty products—some of which were from her friend's small business. Then I did a quick internet search for my name, but only results for other people with the same name, or ones which sounded similar, came up.

Over the coming weeks, I found myself habitually checking her social media accounts, repeatedly looking at the same pictures, tracking her recent movements, and browsing through the accounts of her family and friends. I even learned how to do my eye makeup like hers and bought a satin slip dress to wear to a family member's christening, inspired by the one she wore to her friend's wedding. In conversations with people at work, I tried to imagine the sort of things she might say—even though I'd worked with them for two years without ever really getting to know them much. I'd also bought some of the beauty products from her friend's company, though they caused me to break out, so I ended up binning them.

At some point, I noticed she was often photographed with a guy named Callum, who I recognised from some earlier photos on her account—perhaps a high school acquaintance she'd reconnected with.

Sophie and Callum soon started dating and began sharing posts about their dates, moving in together, and getting a dog. Then, several months later, they went on a mini-break to Paris, where he proposed. There were hundreds of comments on the proposal post, all congratulating the newly engaged couple. Among them was one from Max that read, 'Happy for you, sis.'

A year had passed, and I was fully immersed in Sophie's world. It was somewhere I could go whenever I wanted—if I'd had a bad day or had a spare moment—I thought of it. Except, it wasn't enough. By this point, I felt like I knew Sophie as well as a good friend, but I still hadn't spoken to her.

It was time for me to branch out and start the next chapter of my life. I'd cut ties with my old high school friends, moved on from past relationships, and was taking better care of my health and appearance.

One night, while scrolling through Sophie's social media, I noticed her relationship status had changed to 'single'. She'd written a post thanking everyone for their support during this difficult time. It was a huge shock. I couldn't think of anything that could've caused her and Callum to separate. If they couldn't make it, then no one could.

If there was ever a time to reach out to Sophie, it was during a time of crisis when she needed a shoulder to cry on.

So, I plucked up the courage and decided to message her.

"Hi, Sophie. I hope you don't mind me messaging you out of the blue like this. We've never met, but I know your brother Max and always felt like you and I would get on. I saw you and Callum split up, and I'm so sorry. I'm here if you need to talk x."

A few minutes later, she read the message and replied.

"Sorry, who are you?"

His First Love

Luke and his mother had always been close when he was growing up, and after his father died, their bond only grew stronger. Through the long, dark nights of their grief, they each had a shoulder to cry on. And though the big, old house was quieter and emptier than it had ever been, they both felt reassured by the knowledge that they weren't alone.

He met Ava at the bookshop where she worked, which he liked to frequent on his way to or from work at a marketing agency in the city. They got talking and realised they had quite a lot in common, then exchanged numbers and went on a date a week or so later to a place which did mini golf and burgers.

The date went well—they continued to talk about their shared interests and confided in each other about their past relationships. Luke told her he'd been on dates with other girls here and there but never had anything long-term. She'd had long-term relationships, but none of them had worked out.

While they were walking and talking in the summer evening sun, things took an unexpected turn.

"You're probably gonna think I'm crazy, but... my Mum sometimes sees things, and she drew you," he said, his head lowered.

"Wait, what?" she said, laughing nervously.

"About a month before we met, she drew a picture of you."

"Well, if that isn't the weirdest pick-up line I've ever heard, then I don't know what is."

They both laughed before she said, "But how can you be sure it's me, though? I mean, maybe you've just convinced yourself it's me."

"Maybe it's wishful thinking," he said, smiling. "I'm gonna have to head home soon; my Mum doesn't like to be left alone for too long."

"Oh, sure, no problem," she said. It struck her as odd that a guy in his twenties had a six o'clock curfew because his mother got lonely being by herself at home. But he was kind, and she thought maybe the two of them were just very close, which was surely a good sign. A man who cares about his mother is more likely to care about his girlfriend, she thought to herself before catching herself using the word 'girlfriend' prematurely. It was only the second time they'd met, after all.

"Would you wanna come back with me? I'm sure my Mum wouldn't mind," he said, blushing slightly.

She found herself wondering why he would feel comfortable with a girl he'd only just met, meeting his mother. But then, it seemed to fit in with the rest of his personality—kind and well-meaning, if not a little inexperienced.

"Sure," she said, and the two of them got the train back to the house where he lived with his mother.

It was a large Victorian detached on a quiet road of other similarly sized houses, with long driveways and tall gates distancing them from the hum of cars and commuters taking a shortcut to the train station.

The inside was even more spectacular. There were coloured glass chandeliers hanging from the ceilings, rich tapestries adorning the walls, furniture from bygone eras, souvenirs from faraway places, and the aroma of incense permeated every room.

Luke's mother drifted down the stairs in a loose linen ensemble, her long grey hair in a single plait over her left shoulder, her arms open. She embraced Ava and kissed her on the cheek. "So nice to meet you, Ava. I'm Helena," she said, her mouth smiling but her deep blue eyes wide and alert. As Ava looked into them, she realised she'd never seen anyone with eyes that colour before.

"I've been trying to avoid Joan from number thirty-six all day. She keeps looking in the windows," Helena went on, standing behind the living room door so she wasn't visible through the window.

"Well, we're here now, Mum. No need to worry," Luke said.

Helena told them she would be in her bedroom if they needed anything and disappeared upstairs again, closing the door behind her.

"So, that was Mum," he said.

It was a strange encounter—Helena's somewhat unnatural, performative mannerisms and comments about the neighbour, alongside Luke's cautiousness as he stared blankly while his mother embraced Ava.

The two of them sat on the sofa downstairs and watched one of their favourite sitcoms on TV while getting to know each other more.

"So, you said you and your Mum are close?" she asked, conscious of the fact that during the past few hours, his mother had made several trips back and forth from her bedroom to the kitchen, interrupting them each time to share random thoughts or anecdotes, as if continuing a conversation only she was aware of.

"Yeah. After my Dad passed, we were all each other had," he said pensively.

Luke had said very little about his father—only that he'd died eight years ago from cancer. Sensing he didn't want to open up about this part of his life yet, Ava changed the topic to something more light-hearted, and they carried on talking for another hour or so until they went up to bed.

"Ah, I haven't got any pyjamas with me," Ava said.

As they reached the top of the stairs, Helena came out of her bedroom with a nightshirt in her hands.

"Here, wear this," she said, passing it to Ava.

"Oh, I couldn't."

"Nonsense. You're my guest, and I want you to wear it," she said, already closing the bedroom door as if she wouldn't take no for an answer.

"Thank you, Helena. That's very kind of you."

"Goodnight, you two! Oh, and Luke, don't forget to lock up," Helena called from the other side of the door.

His bedroom was up another flight of stairs in the attic right above his mother's room. It was a warm, humid night—the kind which clings to your skin and hair like a heavy blanket, making every movement slow and difficult, as if the air itself is unwilling to let you go.

As they lay side by side in his bed, both of them felt the comfort of familiarity, as though they'd known each other for not days but years. They each knew they'd found something rare in the other, something to hold onto.

The sound of Helena's low, husky voice rose from her bedroom beneath them. It wasn't clear what she was saying, but as they began drifting off to sleep, her words seemed to melt into the sickly heat until they were nothing more than faded whispers, lost in the warm haze of the night.

The next morning, Ava went downstairs to find Helena making breakfast for her, before insisting she sit at the kitchen table and put whatever she wanted on TV. As she ate her cereal, Helena took a seat across from her. She was slender with delicate features and was sitting in a rather peculiar way, with one of her legs twisted behind the other as she cradled a cup of coffee in her hands.

"I like my coffee black," she said, staring out the kitchen window. "D'you know, you're the first girl Luke's brought back who I've not been able to read?"

Ava felt Helena's dark eyes on her.

"I've had that before. Not from people who see things, just normal people," she said.

"Normal people," Helena repeated, nodding and laughing to herself.

"He said you drew me?" Ava asked, avoiding Helena's intense gaze.

"I did. Luke's probably already told you—I sometimes see things before they happen. It's both a blessing and a curse. I saw my husband's death before it happened. Me and Luke have been lonely ever since, rattling around in this big old house."

Just then, Luke walked into the kitchen and asked if Ava wanted to spend some time together in the city before she went home. She said yes, and the two of them left.

On their way out the door, Helena called down from her bedroom: "Bye, sweetie. Hope to see you again soon."

"Do you think your Mum liked me?" Ava asked Luke as they stood waiting for the train.

"She thinks you're lovely."

"Really? Phew! I was worried she didn't."

"No, trust me, she likes you."

Over the coming weeks, Luke and Ava went on several more dates, often going back to his afterwards. Helena would always be there—she hadn't worked for many years due to ill health. Luke had said it was her nerves and that she struggled to leave the house. She didn't even like family or friends visiting most of the time, though she said she liked having Ava around because the house felt full again.

They bonded over their shared love of books and cooking, and Helena said she was glad to see her son so happy. "She's the daughter I never had," she would say.

When the new year came, however, things changed. Over the past five months, the couple had grown much closer and had started talking about eventually moving in together. Meanwhile, Helena was becoming more reclusive and aloof.

Each time Ava saw her, she couldn't help but notice how little effort she put into maintaining appearances. She would wander around the house semi-naked and leave the bathroom door open while showering. Ava had thought it was perhaps a good sign that Helena felt comfortable being herself while her son's girlfriend was in the house. But sometimes she felt as though Helena got a twisted kind of enjoyment out of flaunting her nakedness. Of course, she hadn't always been that way—when Luke and Ava first started dating, she was always dressed nicely with her hair neatly plaited, and she would often be doing something in the garden or cooking something in the kitchen. But now, she almost never got dressed and wore her hair in loose, messy waves. On nights when Ava stayed over, she would sometimes hear Helena walking around the house at night, her bare feet pounding the wooden floorboards purposefully, while doors slammed and furniture moved. Ava thought Luke must have noticed these behaviours, but he never spoke about them—though she wasn't sure if that was due to familiarity or shame.

One night, while Luke and Ava were chatting on the phone, his voice suddenly went quieter.

"Sorry, can you speak up a bit? I can barely hear you," she said.

"I would, I just don't know if she's listening," he whispered.

"Who?"

"Mum. I think she's at the bottom of my stairs."

She heard him go to close his bedroom door.

"Why would she be listening?" she asked, unnerved.

"I don't know, I just… I think she's afraid of losing me."

"Luke, you have a girlfriend, you're not dead."

"I know, but I think it might be best if we stick to text while we're apart."

Before he hung up, Ava thought she heard Helena's voice in the background. What's wrong with her, can she not stand the idea of her own son having a life? she thought.

Ava wanted to get on with Helena as they had at first, but it was challenging. There were aspects of her personality which she admired—she was intuitive, articulate, strong-minded, and unapologetically honest. She was artistically talented—the lavish and eclectic décor of the house was like a shrine to her abundant creativity. But she could also be obstinate, her convictions sometimes blinding her to other perspectives. And she could be manipulative and cruel—she had a way of blaming others for everything that was wrong with her life, and she loved to play the victim. Things had no doubt been difficult for her after her husband had passed, but they had been difficult for Luke, too, and some of the unkind things Ava had witnessed her say to him cut deeper than the words of someone who was supposed to love him and left scars that went beyond the surface.

Luke kept pleading with Ava to try and make conversation with his mother, but it always felt stilted and forced. Ava could see that beneath Helena's sickly sweet smile, there was a bitterness towards her. She'd tried to engage Helena in conversations about their shared hobbies, but that only went so far, and whenever Ava offered to cook for everyone, Helena was always hovering in the kitchen, giving her exact instructions on how to prepare the food, as though she didn't trust her not to undercook it or lace it with poison.

She began making comments about the way Ava dressed and even left items of clothing out on the bed for her to wear sometimes, but they were nothing like the sort of things she would normally wear and were always inevitably the wrong size. Then Helena would ask her why she wasn't wearing the clothes she left out for her, and Ava would dejectedly tell her they didn't fit, only to be told it was because she was too fat.

On a couple of occasions, Ava had overheard what she assumed were phone conversations between Helena and perhaps one of her friends about the couple. She'd heard her talking about how Luke had 'changed since meeting this girl' and how she felt a 'cold and negative energy' from her.

Around this time, Luke told Ava his mother had started to leave notes around the house for him instead of speaking to him directly.

"I came home from work the other night to a four-page letter about how I hadn't cleaned the dishes properly," he told Ava one Saturday over lunch.

"Do you think she's okay, I mean, mentally?" she asked him.

"To tell you the truth, she's been like this for years, even before my dad died. They almost got divorced a few times while I was growing up. Me and her used to be so close when I was a kid, and now it's like she can't stand the sight of me. Yet, she's always complaining that I don't spend enough time with her," Luke said.

"I'm worried it's my fault," Ava said.

"It's not your fault; you're great. It's Mum."

"What should we do?"

"Move out. It's about time I stood on my own two feet. She has enough money. She'll manage. And besides, I'm not her keeper."

"Where will you live?"

"Let's move in together," he said, reaching for her hand across the table.

Ava thought about his proposition. He was different from any other guy she'd dated—he accepted her for who she was, and she did the same for him in return. They truly loved and cared for each other and couldn't let his mother stand in their way. And aside from the urgency of his domestic situation, she did see a future with him.

They hatched a plan to start looking for somewhere to rent, which would give both of them a short commute to work. Within a fortnight, they found somewhere which, although not perfect, would suit their needs. They put a deposit down and began preparing for the move. Meanwhile, Ava continued to see Luke, sometimes going back to his mother's house, saying nothing of their plan to move in together.

One night, as she passed Helena's room on her way back from the bathroom, Ava heard her say:

"You know, a boy's first love is his mother."

Through the gap in the door, which was partly open, Ava could see she was sitting on the edge of her bed with only the moonlight illuminating her silver hair. Half asleep, she didn't respond and tiptoed along the landing and up the stairs to Luke's room in the attic, hoping Helena didn't hear her. But she did, and a few minutes later, they heard her quick, deliberate footsteps coming up the stairs.

Then came three loud knocks on the other side of the door.

The couple remained silent. Then came another three loud knocks.

"Mum, please just go back to bed," Luke said.

She huffed and went back downstairs to her bedroom. Perturbed, the couple talked about what had just happened in hushed tones.

"I don't think I can put up with this for much longer," Ava said.

"We'll be moving soon and this will all be over. But until then, maybe you should stay away from here. I don't want anything bad to happen."

"Don't you see it? This is exactly what she wants—you stuck here."

"Let her think what she wants; we know it isn't true. We'll be away from this madness soon, I promise."

For the next couple of weeks, Ava stayed away from the house, and only spoke to Luke over text. He told her things were still tense there but that he was glad she was out of it for her sake.

As the moving day approached, they made arrangements for a van to transport their belongings to the new place. The night before, she texted him.

Are we still on for 12 tomorrow?

She waited for him to read the message and for the three little dots to say he was typing to follow. Nothing.

She tried calling, but it went straight to voicemail. Then she began to worry.

In desperation, she made her way to his place. When she got there, she could see some of the upstairs lights were on, but downstairs was dark.

She let herself in and made her way along the hall towards the stairs and then heard a single creak from one of the floorboards behind her. She stopped, looking back towards the dark kitchen.

"Luke, is that you?" she asked nervously before trying to call his phone again.

She heard his muffled ringtone somewhere in the house.

"Luke?" she called again. Then she heard the sound of bare feet shuffling across the kitchen floor. She turned back again towards the kitchen and saw Helena emerging from the shadows.

"Oh, Helena, you gave me a fright. I didn't see you. Do you know where Luke is? I've been trying to call him, but he isn't answering."

"Oopsy daisy," she said, pulling Luke's phone out of her pocket and dropping it on the floor.

She began walking towards Ava, slowly.

"Helena, I know we haven't always seen eye to eye, but I'd be really grateful if you could just tell me where Luke is," Ava said.

"He's at home with his mother, where he belongs," Helena said.

"Is he upstairs? Luke!" Ava stepped back towards the foot of the stairs, her eyes fixed on Helena, who was still at the other end of the hall.

"A boy's first love is his mother; I told you that, but you didn't listen. He doesn't want you," Helena said.

Her left hand had been behind her back the whole time. Looking in the glass of the kitchen door behind her, Ava saw something glinting in her hand—a long, sharp kitchen knife. Horrified, she turned and bolted up the stairs, calling Luke's name as she went.

As she reached the top, she heard Luke's voice—drowsy, slow, and thick with sleep—from his mother's room. She rushed in and found him lying atop the crumpled bed covers on his side, his arm hanging down, a crimson gash on his temple.

"Luke, wake up, wake up! She's got a knife!" she cried, shaking him. Helena was now halfway up the stairs, holding the knife out in front of her.

"Help me up," Luke said, staggering upright and heading for the doorway as Helena reached the top of the stairs.

"Sweetie, you're awake. I was just about to call you down for dinner," she said, her tone soft and gentle.

"Mum, this has got to stop. We need to get you some help," Luke said. "Now, give me the knife."

She pointed the blade at herself, stepping backwards.

"Mum, come on, you don't need to do this."

"Ever since you were a little boy, you promised me you'd always be there," she said, tears in her eyes.

"And I will be, but I have to go my own way. Everyone does."

"Listen to this," she said, gesturing towards him, laughing. "You've been putting ideas in his head, you bitch. That was your plan all along—to take him away from me. But he'll never love you the way he loves me." She smiled, pointing the knife into her chest once more.

"Mum, no!" Luke cried, grabbing her arm and prying the knife from her grip. As she tried to push him away, she stumbled and fell down the stairs.

Months later, Luke stared at his mother in her chair across the room, his eyes tired, hollow.

"I'm feeling a bit hungry. Should we have dinner soon?" he said.

"Yes. But I don't feel up to making it. Would you?" she said.

He stood and went into the kitchen, his limbs feeling heavy and aching with each step. As he was about to open the fridge, his eyes fell on a small photo held on by a magnet—it was of him and Ava at the mini-golf place from their first date, smiling. He'd left it there to remind himself of better times, but it was bittersweet to look at.

That single photo contained an alternative future—a brighter one where he wasn't trapped in the cage he'd chosen for himself. Above all else, that's what hurt the most—that he'd chosen the life he now had. He caught himself thinking that if things had been different—if his father hadn't died, if his mother could have handled the loss, or if he had just listened to Ava from the start—maybe he wouldn't be in the mess he was now. But regret wouldn't save him; it would only eat him up from the inside. So, he had to convince himself this was where he belonged—at home with his mother. Ava had probably moved on by now.

When the food was ready, he brought his mother's plate into the living room and set it down on a tray in front of her.

"It's a good thing I've got you by my side," she said.

"Always, Mum."

Such Delicate Hands

"Will you write a song about me?" he asked in that playful yet condescending tone she disliked, reclining against the headboard of the bed.

"Maybe," she said with a nervous laugh, reaching for the remote control on the nightstand and turning the TV on. A kids' cartoon flickered to life; she didn't bother changing the channel. He didn't know she had already written one about him, though she refused to give him the satisfaction of knowing. She didn't want him to think he had broken through the cold exterior he hated so much because he couldn't bear her rejection. No one could break it. She lived in her interior world, where nothing could hurt her.

This was the second time they'd met at a sordid hotel near the train station of the small town they were both from, though he'd lived elsewhere for most of his adult life. She'd escaped briefly to go to university, where she'd been sold the dream of becoming more than someone from her hometown could ever hope to be, but unemployment had dragged her back.

Returning to something you once broke free from is all the more bitter once you've tasted something sweet. Yet there she was, spending her Sunday afternoon with a man who had left his eight-year-old daughter's birthday party for a secret rendezvous with a girl less than half his age.

He was in his late forties, short with a middle-aged spread, a thick beard, and glasses. This was how he'd looked for as long as she'd known him—only the years had made him greyer, while she had improved with age.

She'd been neighbours with his mother all her life and he'd been her piano teacher during her teenage years. Seven years earlier, he'd moved her fingers to the right keys while she played, and her heart had fluttered in her chest as she felt his hands touch hers.

After his mother died, he came back to clear the house out and bumped into her one day, while putting things in the boot of his car. He'd invited her out to dinner, knowing what he wanted early on, though he wasn't entirely convinced she'd give it to an old man like him. She'd accepted, thinking it'd be nice to catch up, even though she'd had a different feeling about him ever since the piano lessons.

At dinner, she'd sat across the table from him, half repulsed, half infatuated, listening as he gushed about how "smart" and "fascinating" she was. And how she had "such delicate hands" with "long, slender fingers." As he spoke, she watched his sad, drooping eyes behind the glasses, almost able to smell the desperation on his breath.

It was like meeting a celebrity crush and realising they aren't as appealing as they look on camera, while still being in awe of their presence. She didn't find him attractive, but then, it wasn't him she loved; it was that he saw something in her.

She knew he had a wife and daughter, but tried not to think about it; convincing herself that there was more to it than she knew. Perhaps they weren't together anymore and just stuck around for the sake of their child. In any case, he was there with her and a part of her selfishly enjoyed the attention. Or maybe she was desperately lonely.

"Perhaps it's getting a little too real for you," he'd said when she'd hesitated after the first time he booked a hotel room for them one night after work. And perhaps he was right, because it was easy to get caught up in the fantasy of him and her in her head. But in the cold light of that Sunday afternoon, she felt like a stranger to herself. If this was the price of attention, connection, desire, or friendship—because she wasn't even sure what she wanted from him anymore—then she would have to pay it.

Their bodies were incongruous—his old and hers young. All the time he was pawing over her, she was somewhere else, somewhere beyond that dismal hotel room, in the safety of her interior world.

It was a cheap hotel, with a tacky neon sign and fake palm trees marking its entrance. Inside were numerous squalid rooms with outdated decor, the air thick with artificial air freshener and cigarette smoke. It was the sort of place that only commuters or those with business they'd rather keep quiet stayed at.

"You're so frigid, you're like a dead person," he told her, disdain in his voice, as she sat cross-legged on the end of the bed, watching TV blankly. It was the only thing she could look at in the room to avoid looking at him.

"Maybe I should go," she said, beginning to question why she'd lied to her family about where she was hurrying off to on such a rainy day just to meet a man who compared her to a corpse.

"No, don't go. I want to show you something," he said, reaching for his phone. "I'm teaching Clara to play piano."

A video of Clara's small fingers dancing over the keys, a look of deep concentration on her face, came on screen.

"Watch her hands," he said.

She played each note with delicate precision, her body swaying ever so slightly with the rhythm, as the upbeat melody filled the gloomy hotel room. When she'd finished, she turned and smiled proudly at the camera.

Suddenly, she felt overwhelmed by it all—by him, herself, what they'd done, and the fact that his daughter would be blowing out her birthday candles, wishing her dad was there.

Ruins

The newlyweds' first home was a little stone cottage named Am Byth, nestled in the foothills of a Welsh mountain range. Captured by its fairy tale charm, Renee's husband Miles had set his heart on it from the moment he'd found it just a short way from an archaeological dig he was working on.

The remote area was rumoured to have had a fort and an adjoining settlement back in the 1200s, though no physical evidence had yet been found. Old maps and handwritten records, held at the library archives in the nearest town, were the only known remnants of what had once been. Not well known, no one had taken it upon themselves to learn the history of the castle and what had become of it, until an eager group of academics stumbled upon it and thought it might prove to be a fascinating research project.

One of these academics was Miles, who also had a vested interest in the project—hoping that the peace and tranquillity of the countryside would do him and his wife the world of good. She could set up an artist's retreat, and he could write about the local history. She wasn't convinced that moving somewhere so far away from the lives they knew would solve any of the problems they'd already encountered after just six months of marriage. But she had to admit that city life was becoming too expensive to sustain and that the countryside offered a much simpler way of life.

They'd been married for less than a month when family and friends had started to ask when they were going to "settle down", though Renee could never understand the sense of urgency others felt about her biological clock. She and Miles had met at university, while she was studying fine art and he was studying ancient history. They'd spent their twenties together, each pursuing their own ambitions, yet always returning to one another at the end of the day. But marriage had changed things—it required sacrifice and compromise. It signified the end of an era and the beginning of another. As she approached thirty and saw her friends become parents, the question of whether she and her husband loomed on the horizon.

It had come up in conversation before, here and there. When they were on a trip to the Lakes one summer, he'd said how he'd like to go there as a family someday. But he hadn't said anything like that in a while, and she was beginning to wonder if he'd changed his mind. Though she didn't bring it up, because she wasn't entirely sure about the matter herself.

They bought the cottage at auction for a low price, since it had been derelict for several years after the previous owner had passed away. When summer came, they packed their belongings into the car and made the three-hour-long journey to their new life.

Renee had suffered with travel sickness for as long as she could remember. As she sat in the passenger seat, gazing out of the car window at the rolling hills, her stomach turned with each bend in the winding mountain road. Though there were no buildings for miles around, the monotone landscape had a claustrophobia of its own. Since there were no landmarks, there was no sense of time, no destination in sight.

When they finally arrived, the cottage was even more isolated than she'd imagined. The road stopped at the bottom of a dirt path, which led up to a small walled garden that had once been well-kept but was now overgrown. In one of its corners stood a wooden birdhouse, covered by a dark curtain of ivy, and inside it was the pottery figure of a hooded man pushing a wheelbarrow.

The cottage was built from grey stone. It had a slate roof, a heavy wooden front door, and a pair of symmetrical windows on either side. And growing on a trellis arched over the doorway was a purple wisteria, which had wrapped its vines around the frame, creating a cascade of flowers that gently swayed in the breeze. It certainly is idyllic, Renee thought, as they began carrying boxes up the garden path.

Inside the house, the décor was shabby and antiquated but still retained an air of homeliness. Though the majority of its contents had been cleared by auctioneers, some furniture remained. In the living room was a threadbare armchair, a writing bureau, and a wooden footstool. And in the master bedroom upstairs was a cast-iron bed and a dressing table with a mirror.

The couple spent the evening arranging their belongings in the house and then helping the men from the removals firm carry heavier items of furniture. They ate tinned soup, since there was no working oven or fridge, and went to bed just after midnight.

The following day, while Miles was doing research at the library in the local town, Renee began the arduous task of sorting through the decades of clutter in the outhouse, which she planned to repurpose as her art studio.

The last owner was an elderly woman with no surviving relatives to inherit the souvenirs of a lifetime. She'd been a collector of everything from old postcards to post-mortem photography—the latter of which proved to be morbidly fascinating and kept Renee occupied for several hours as she leafed through the mildewed pages of Victorian albums filled with vacant-eyed elders and sleeping infants dressed in their Sunday best. Loved ones enshrined in flowers, resting with secrets upon their lips. *Who were these people, and how had their pictures ended up in this outhouse?* she wondered.

Once Renee had finished sorting through everything in the outhouse, she went for a walk in the wild, untamed forest that backed onto the cottage. She made her own way, since there were no paths to follow that had already been trodden by others.

There seemed to be two distinct areas of the forest. There was an outer ring of trees and then a central cluster, which grew on a steep slope, towering above the cottage. She started to climb it, using rocks and branches to pull herself up, but before she could get any further, it began to rain. She remembered Miles telling her that the elements were much more unpredictable up in the mountains than they were down below, and that a light shower could turn into a thunderstorm at a moment's notice, so she turned around and made her way back towards the house.

As she descended the slope, her footsteps cushioned by the soft forest floor, she had the peculiar feeling of having been there before. Perhaps in a dream or a childhood memory, she thought. But how? She had no knowledge of the place before Miles had come to her that Monday evening with his idea to buy the empty cottage.

When she reached the bottom of the slope, she went straight into the outhouse, where she began preparing some paints and a canvas on an easel. As she made quick, broad strokes with the brush, adding layer upon layer of paint, a scene began to emerge. Where the canvas was once white, there was now a painting of a castle on a misty hilltop, enclosed by trees. Its palette of blues, greys, and browns blended together softly, giving it an ethereal quality—one which Renee found herself both frightened and fascinated by, like the landscape on her own doorstep.

Where did that come from? she asked herself, stepping back from the painting to find that her clothes and the floor were covered in paint. It was as if someone had taken control of her and brought their vision to life through her eyes and hands.

She took the wet painting into the house, where she put it on the floor against the wall at the end of their bed. Then she went downstairs into the kitchen, where she looked at the clock and realised several hours had passed. Miles would be home soon. She hadn't heard from him all day, but she hadn't felt worried or alone in their new, unfamiliar surroundings.

It was starting to get dark by the time Miles came home and found her sitting in the threadbare armchair in the living room, sketching something. She felt him standing over her and looked up.

"What have you been up to today?" he asked, taking his hat and coat off.

"Not much. I went for a walk. Oh, and then I painted something," she said lethargically.

"Sounds like you've not stopped. What's this?" he said, pointing to the drawing in her lap.

She looked down at the charcoal forms appearing on the page, which looked like a hill surrounded by tall trees casting long shadows in the moonlight.

As she stood in the living room doorway while he talked about his day, her mind wandered to the forest on the hill. *Why did it feel so familiar?* she thought.

"Anyway, I'll see you upstairs," he said, leaving the room.

When they got into bed, he fell asleep almost instantly. It took her a little longer, but as she listened to his slow, gentle breathing, while staring at the moonlit painting of the castle, she fell into a deep sleep.

That night, she dreamt of a castle. Below the hilltop on which it stood was a small village of cylindrical dwellings made from wood and clay, which had pointed straw roofs. Among them, shawled women stoked fires, while men pushed wooden carts, and children followed them like shadows. The smell of roasting meat mingled with the smoke from the fires that rose into the cold night, carried by the breeze.

Renee had been watching all this from a chamber, somewhere hidden within the castle, which was adorned with heavy tapestries, woven with threads of crimson, gold, and green. She was embroidering something by firelight—an enchanting scene, with a white stag in the centre of a forest clearing. Then, while pushing the needle up from underneath the fabric, she pricked her finger and awoke with a start.

The room was dark, apart from the pale moonlight filtering through the curtains, and Miles lay sleeping soundly on the other side of the bed. She looked at her fingertip where she'd felt a sharp sting as the needle pierced the skin—there was a tiny bead of blood there. She looked at the painting at the end of the bed—something about it had changed. She cast her eyes over it, taking in the trees, the stone walls, the pointed towers. It was all still there, just more weathered and craggy than she had initially painted it.

Is it possible I've started sleepwalking again? she wondered. It had been years since she had; the last time was during a family holiday, when she was still a teenager. She'd left the hotel room and gone down to the beach. Her father had woken up and realised she wasn't there just in time to stop her from walking into the sea.

She pulled the bedcover up to her chin and closed her eyes, trying to push the thought aside. The next time she woke, it was morning. The noise of metal pots and pans clanging together drifted up from downstairs, as Miles prepared breakfast. When she went down, he was making a pot of coffee.

"There's some poached eggs there for you," he said, pouring her a cup of coffee, before placing it beside the plate of eggs.

"Thank you," she said, taking a seat. He was leaning against the counter, eating a piece of toast. "Miles, do you think it's possible the castle you're looking for is on the hill behind our house?"

"I mean, it's not impossible, but there are lots of hills around here—in theory, it could be on any of them."

"It's just... last night I dreamt of a castle on a hill, with a village below it, and it reminded me of the hill behind our house."

"You and your fantasies—always away with the fairies," he said, laughing, before ruffling her hair as he went to pour himself some coffee.

"But I really think there's something there," she said, turning to face him. "Maybe you should check it out."

"Maybe. I'll mention it to the team, see what they think. I was planning on doing a bit of writing today about one of the old slate mines in the valley," he said.

"Oh, nice," Renee said, her mind beginning to wander again.

"Well, actually, it had a pretty bad reputation for all the fatalities that happened there during the height of its operation." He paused, waiting for her response. "Renee?"

"Sorry, what?"

"I'll be in the study if you need me. I think you should get some rest; you seem out of it," he said before rinsing his cup in the sink and leaving the kitchen.

Renee sat there for a few more minutes, looking out the window at the overgrown grass in the back garden, as she sipped her coffee. She knew exactly what she was going to do with her day—she was going to paint her dream from the night before.

Gathering paints and brushes from the outhouse, Renee brought them into the cottage and up to their bedroom. It's time to breathe some life back into this place, she thought, as she began painting the faint outline of an arrow slit on the wall.

Several hours later, Miles came out of the study and went into the bedroom to find Renee adding some trees into the mural she'd painted on the far wall, at the end of the bed. To his astonishment, she'd turned the plain, white wall spotted with mould into a medieval tower made from grey stone, with a single arched window where the real window was, and two arrow slits either side of it. Through the arrow slits was a view of hills and trees, with mountains, which were just about visible, in the distance.

"Renee...," he said, lost for words. "I had no idea you were planning this."

"I wasn't, it just sort of happened," she said, climbing down from the ladder she had been using to reach the upper part of the wall.

"It's... I mean, I'm not sure it's what most couples have in their bedroom, but it could work," he said.

"This is what I saw in my dream last night. I was sitting in a tower like this, watching the world go by. And d'you know, the crazy thing is—I pricked my finger on a needle in the dream, and when I woke up, it was bleeding."

"Huh. Do you think you've been sleepwalking again?"

"No. Well... I don't think so."

"We'd better keep an eye on it, after what happened last time. Your dad was close to putting a lock on your bedroom door."

"Yeah, well, he overreacts. Don't worry; it won't happen again."

It was early evening by the time Renee had finished painting the mural. Hungry and exhausted, she ate dinner and then went to bed, shortly followed by Miles. This time she fell asleep right away and slipped into a deep sleep.

Once again, she dreamt of the castle. But this time, she was roaming its long, dimly lit passages, perhaps in search of something or someone who wasn't there. She was weeping because she couldn't find them. All the while, the castle seemed to be falling down around her, as she went from one corridor to the next. Then she came to the longest and darkest of them all—it had a door at the end of it, with a heavy iron handle which she struggled to lift.

She woke weeping. Miles, who had been fast asleep, heard her cries and turned the bedside lamp on to see what was wrong.

"Renee, what's happened?" he asked, concern in his eyes.

"It's nothing. I... I had a dream about the castle again, but it was falling down around me, and I didn't know what to do," she said, covering her face with her hands.

"Ah, sweetheart. It was just a dream, nothing to worry about. You're safe here, with me."

"But it felt so real. There was a door—I was trying to open it, but it wouldn't open. And I had this feeling that there was something awful behind it, something I didn't want to see, but which I had to. And then it all went black."

He exhaled, rubbing her back between her shoulder blades. "You stay right there; I'll bring you some tea," he said.

She knew he meant well, but he hadn't heard the whole story—she hadn't shared with him what she found behind the door, the true reason behind her tears.

"Here you go," he said, handing her a hot cup of tea. "You'll have forgotten it all by morning."

Over the next couple of nights, Renee tried to stay awake for as long as she could, for fear of falling asleep and dreaming of the crumbling castle again. She sat in bed drawing or reading—doing anything to distract herself—for hours on end, surrounded by the safety of the room's four walls; the mural of the castle a reminder of how beautiful it had once been.

"You can't stay up all night, you'll make yourself ill," Miles told her on the third night he found her wide awake in the early hours of the morning. But she paid him no notice, continuing to read by lamplight, even though it was almost half two in the morning.

"Do you mind? Just because you don't want to sleep, doesn't mean I don't," he said, turning away from her and pulling the bedcovers over his head.

She got up and went downstairs into the living room, where she curled up on the armchair and read until her eyelids grew heavy, the words began to blend together, and eventually, she fell asleep.

The castle appeared to her, once more—its stone walls tumbling down around her, as she walked down the long, dark passage towards the door. This time, it opened by itself. She hesitated, not wanting to pass the threshold. But before she had time to think, the floor began to shift beneath her feet, and she was forced to leap forwards or fall.

There it was—the thing she feared most. At the centre of the empty room stood a large, round mirror. As she stepped towards it, a beam of sunlight coming in through the window got caught in its glass and was reflected all around the room. She saw herself staring back, and as the mirror cracked in two, she noticed a second shadow appear on the floor in front of her. She looked back at the mirror; there was a woman standing beside her.

The woman looked to be in her early to mid-twenties, with a pale, sallow complexion. She was wearing a long, ivory-coloured dress with billowing sleeves. Her hair was in braids, almost reaching her waist. And her face was familiar. Renee recognised the same bone structure and searching look in her own face. She'd seen this woman before in other dreams she'd had in her childhood and, once or twice, in her bedroom mirror. She always appeared before times of great change or tragedy. The first time Renee had seen her was the night before her grandmother's death when she was only six years old. Though it was only her face and not her full body—until now. She'd never told anyone about her, half out of hope she was just a figment of her imagination, half out of fear she wasn't.

Plucking up the courage, Renee asked her, "Who are you?"

"I am thee of another lyf," she said, her voice seeming to echo from far away, although she was right there.

"What? How is that even possible, and why now? Is something bad going to happen?"

"Thee knoweth the answers, yet 'tis thou who guideth thee unto them."

"But I don't know them; please tell me."

"Lo, these shattered walls, once proud and strong, now crumble 'neath the weight of time—so too did the bonds we once held dear, unravelling 'til naught remains but dust and shadow."

She thought of Miles back at home in bed, and then remembered she wasn't really in the castle, but in a dream. Willing herself to wake up, she became aware of a cold, wet sensation spreading from her feet to her legs, and then to the rest of her body. She awoke to find herself standing barefoot in a grassy clearing on top of the hill behind the cottage. The sun was rising, and about fifty feet in front of her were the weathered remains of a castle— a once formidable structure, now a haunting spectre of its former glory. Walking towards the remains, with her back to Renee, was the woman whose reflection she'd seen in the mirror.

This can't be real, she thought, pinching the skin on her arm between her thumb and forefinger, but nothing happened. It wasn't a dream anymore—it was real.

Having entered the castle through the collapsed doorway, her doppelgänger was now climbing the stairs of one of the castle's four towers, which had a single arched window at the top of it. Renee watched intently as the woman stepped onto the ledge of the window, her pallid complexion and ivory gown making her appear like a ghostly apparition in the dim light of the early morning. She stood on the ledge for seemingly a lifetime before putting out her left foot.

"Wait, don't!" Renee called, as she began running towards the castle entrance.

But before she could get there, the woman stepped off the ledge, plummeting—ever so slowly, as if in a dream—towards the Earth below. The moment her body touched the ground, she vanished, as though swallowed by the very air.

Bewildered, Renee dropped to her hands and knees, running her palms over the damp grass, as if to make sure she hadn't lost her mind. But there was no sign of the woman.

Perhaps she never left the castle and is still inside, she thought, wandering through its tall, shadowy doorway.

Immediately to her left was another dark opening, which led to a narrow spiral staircase. She began climbing it, her bare feet against the cold, hard stone. When she reached the top, she saw the same window—the deep orange sunrise on the horizon casting a shadow of the castle on the grass below it. She stepped onto the ledge and looked over it, expecting to see the pale woman, but instead, saw Miles.

"Renee, wait!" he cried, a desperate look on his face.

She stumbled backwards, then heard his frantic footsteps ascending the staircase before he appeared in the doorway.

"I woke up and you weren't there," he said, panting for breath. "I had a feeling you'd be here."

"Miles, you have to believe me—something really weird is happening. I've been having dreams and visions of this place for days. I saw something really bad and I'm scared."

He walked towards her and embraced her in a hug. The warmth of it pulled her back to reality, reminding her of those halcyon days of their early twenties. Despite the passage of time, they were both still there.

"You were right," he said. "The castle was right here all along."

185

The Lady by the Lake

"There's a scary old lady by the lake," Niall said, peering through the slats in the living room blinds.

"That's nice. Now, come and eat your breakfast. We have to be at school in fifteen minutes," his mother called from the kitchen.

He stayed at the window a moment longer, his eyes drawn to the frail figure of an elderly woman with pale yellow hair, hung in limp strands around her head, sitting on the bench beside the lake. She was wearing a long, plastic raincoat and was clutching a small handbag in her lap. Her face was hidden behind a veil of hair, but she seemed lost in thought as her gaze lingered on the lake.

"We're going to be late, now hurry!" his mother called again from the kitchen.

Niall gulped down his cereal, then pulled on his school jumper and grabbed his bag from the hall stand on the way out the door.

As the car pulled out of the driveway, he noticed the woman wasn't there anymore. He wondered if she had gone inside one of the houses. She wasn't down the lane, and it would have been impossible for her to get away so quickly.

There was only one way to get in and out of Gossamer Lane, which was a cul-de-sac at the end of a long, winding road, with ten houses arranged in the shape of a horseshoe around a lake. Though the layer of green algae floating on the lake's surface, and the thick, sticky mud surrounding it, made it more like a swamp.

Sometimes, Niall and his friends would play by it, capturing pond skaters and tadpoles with little fishing nets. Or they'd throw stones into it to see who could make the biggest splash.

When Niall got home from school that day, he asked his mother if he could play out with his best friend, Theo, who lived three doors down.

It was autumn, and the sun was hidden behind the clouds. A gentle breeze stirred the fallen leaves, sweeping them into swirling piles. And all was quiet on the lane, except for squeaking moorhens, foraging for food on the lake.

"Make sure you're back by six or your dinner will go cold," his mother said as he left the house.

Theo was on his bike at the end of the driveway. The two boys went down the lane to a small wooded area, where they pretended to be intrepid jungle explorers, hunting dangerous and exotic animals, such as the Deadly Swamp Snake. Theo was convinced he'd seen one of these in the lake, but no one believed anything he said since he claimed to have seen a black wolf in his father's gardening shed last summer.

As the sky grew darker, the boys made their way back up the lane. Theo went home, but as Niall neared the driveway of his house, he noticed the woman sitting on the bench by the lake again.

He thought she looked lonely, sat all by herself, so he decided to approach her. As he got closer, he saw she was taking bright red berries out of her handbag and throwing them into the lake for the birds. She turned to face him with a smile.

"Hello, there. What's your name?" she said.

Her bony frame and croaky voice made him fearful of moving any closer. "My name's Niall. What's yours?" he said.

"Oo, what a nice name you have. I'm Hazel. Come, sit," she said, patting the empty seat beside her.

He reluctantly sat down and watched as she continued to delve into her handbag for berries with her gnarled fingers.

"What are those?" he asked.

"They're rowan berries—the birds love 'em. And they're good for warding off evil," she rasped.

"Evil?" he asked.

"There are some dark things in this world. Very dark, indeed. And not everything is as it seems. Sometimes, the things we fear aren't all that bad, and it's the things we don't notice which we ought to be afraid of," she said, tossing some berries into the lake.

"Here, take some for the birds and some for protection," she said, placing a handful in his palm.

He threw a few into the lake and put the rest in his pocket, before remembering his mother wanted him home in time for dinner.

"I have to go now. Maybe we'll see each other again if you live nearby," he said.

"Oh, I hope so. I'm not far, not far at all."

As he walked away, he wondered about the dark things she spoke of, and whether Theo was telling the truth about the black wolf he'd seen in his father's shed. And he thought that perhaps Hazel wasn't so bad after all, even though he'd thought she looked mean and scary to begin with. He reached into his pocket and rolled one of the berries she'd given him between his thumb and forefinger—it felt cold and hard. As he reached the front door to his house, he turned around to wave goodbye, but saw she had vanished.

She probably wasn't far, though. Not far at all.